108課綱、全民英檢中級適用

# 30天計畫：
# 打造 核心 英文字彙題本

丁雍嫻 邢雯桂 盧思嘉 應惠蕙 編著

附解析本

**丁雍嫻**
學歷／國立臺灣師範大學英語學系學士
　　　國立臺灣師範大學英語學系研究所暑期班
經歷／國立新竹女子高級中學

**邢雯桂**
學歷／國立中央大學英美語文學系學士
　　　美國新罕布夏大學英語教學碩士
經歷／國立新竹女子高級中學

**盧思嘉**
學歷／國立彰化師範大學英語學系學士
　　　英國伯明罕大學英語教學碩士
經歷／國立新竹女子高級中學

**應惠蕙**
學歷／國立臺灣師範大學英語學系學士
　　　國立臺灣師範大學英語學系碩士
經歷／國立新竹女子高級中學
　　　華東臺商子女學校

三民書局

# 序

英語 Make Me High 系列的理想在於超越，在於創新。

這是時代的精神，也是我們出版的動力；

這是教育的目的，也是我們進步的執著。

針對英語的全球化與未來的升學趨勢，

我們設計了一系列適合普高、技高學生的英語學習書籍。

面對英語，不會徬徨不再迷惘，學習的心徹底沸騰，

心情好 High！

實戰模擬，掌握先機知己知彼，百戰不殆決勝未來，

分數更 High！

選擇優質的英語學習書籍，才能激發學習的強烈動機；

興趣盎然便不會畏懼艱難，自信心要自己大聲說出來。

本書如良師指引循循善誘，如益友相互鼓勵攜手成長。

展書輕閱，你將發現……

學習英語原來也可以這麼 High！

# 前　言

　　《30 天計畫：打造核心英文字彙題本》乃根據大考中心高中英文參考詞彙表之 4500 個字彙範圍， 由作者群模擬大考題型精心編寫而成。全書共分 30 回，每回 30 題，題型包括以下三大類型：

Ⅰ. Multiple Choice（字彙選擇，20 題）

　　測驗學生對英文單句的理解程度及各單字的熟悉度。

Ⅱ. Fill in the Blank（字彙填空，5 題）

　　評量學生對詞組及慣用語的運用程度。

Ⅲ. Guided Translation（引導式翻譯，5 題）

　　檢視學生是否能靈活運用單字、片語，進而將其運用於句子內。

　　透過這些題型，將可由點、線、面全方位檢核學生的字彙實力。

　　本手冊的使用方式不拘。學生可先研讀三民出版的《基礎英文字彙力 2000》、《核心英文字彙力 2001~4500》，於熟悉各單字之用法後，再以本書驗收學習成果 ；亦可直接利用本書， 於學測前 30 天寫題衝刺，檢視較不熟悉的字詞，並利用其他工具書（如字典）的輔助，擴增自己的字彙。無論何種方式，相信皆能增強讀者們的字彙能力。

　　字彙乃語文之本，能通曉各單字的意義、掌握重要單字的用法，則各式題型的測驗皆不足為懼。期望本書能對正在準備考試的莘莘學子們有所助益。

# Table of Contents

練習完一個回次後，你可以在該回次的◯打勾並在 12/31 填寫完成日期。

・圖片來源：Shutterstock

# Round 1

## I. Multiple Choice

(　　) 1. Lena attempted to save her puppy when it _____, but unfortunately, it still lost its life.
(A) choked　　　(B) completed　　(C) bankrupted　　(D) confronted

(　　) 2. The mayor declared his support for reforms to _____ criticism from the government officials.
(A) pollute　　　(B) bandage　　(C) prolong　　(D) counter

(　　) 3. The kids needed several _____ of paper to draw pictures in the art class.
(A) sheets　　　(B) loaves　　(C) slices　　(D) jars

(　　) 4. The study indicates that the disease is caused by a defective _____ rather than germs.
(A) gene　　　(B) birth　　(C) design　　(D) medium

(　　) 5. The cruise ship was sinking fast after hitting an iceberg, so the captain gave the order to _____ it.
(A) disclose　　　(B) abandon　　(C) drown　　(D) absorb

(　　) 6. The tourists felt upset because the violent storm _____ their vacation on the tropical island.
(A) spared　　　(B) spoiled　　(C) spun　　(D) splashed

(　　) 7. After the surgery, it didn't take long for the patient's wound to _____ up.
(A) cure　　　(B) consult　　(C) heal　　(D) infect

( ) 8. After Ben's house was broken into, the police asked him to make a list of the missing _____.
(A) articles      (B) matters      (C) events      (D) circles

( ) 9. Instead of _____ himself on those who had ever bullied him, the boy decided to forgive and forget.
(A) reinforcing      (B) revising      (C) reviewing      (D) revenging

( ) 10. The company _____ hundreds of job applicants. However, only a few people applied for the position.
(A) transformed      (B) decided      (C) anticipated      (D) proved

( ) 11. A happy marriage must be based on _____ respect and understanding between a couple.
(A) common      (B) double      (C) academic      (D) mutual

( ) 12. The customer paid for her meal with a one-hundred-dollar _____.
(A) paper      (B) bill      (C) bank      (D) pill

( ) 13. The smell of salt in the air _____ that the sea was not far away.
(A) advocated      (B) remarked      (C) commanded      (D) suggested

( ) 14. _____ disturbed, Chloe couldn't focus on whatever she's doing and kept thinking of the painful breakup.
(A) Generally      (B) Emotionally      (C) Logically      (D) Frankly

( ) 15. Any language that carries meaning of sexual or racial discrimination will be considered _____.
(A) educational      (B) destructive      (C) respectful      (D) offensive

( ) 16. The newly-built baseball stadium has a seating _____ of fifty thousand.
(A) capacity      (B) reservation      (C) responsibility      (D) tragedy

( ) 17. Nowadays, a growing number of people are _____ to their smartphones. Some people just can't live without them.
(A) vulnerable      (B) addicted      (C) desirable      (D) anxious

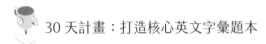

(     ) 18. Adequate healthcare _____ in this mountainous area are still lacking.

(A) compositions    (B) charities     (C) facilities     (D) boundaries

(     ) 19. Young people tend to share their secrets with their _____ rather than with their parents.

(A) pupils      (B) matches     (C) peers      (D) companies

(     ) 20. The fashion designer writes a monthly _____ on current fashion trends for the fashion magazine.

(A) colony      (B) code       (C) column      (D) copy

## II. Fill in the Blank （從下方選出適合字彙做適當變化，填入答案）

| burn | disguise | length | account | absence |
|------|----------|--------|---------|---------|

_____ 1. I hope my boss will take into _____ the fact that I was ill when giving the presentation.

_____ 2. Missing my plane was a blessing in _____ because the plane crashed just after takeoff.

_____ 3. The sailor spoke at _____ about his adventures and near-death experiences at sea.

_____ 4. After the war, the victims came back to find that their houses had _____ down.

_____ 5. We decided to offer the job to Mr. Baker in the _____ of other better applicants.

## III. Guided Translation （寫出完整字彙）

1. 由於公司損失很多錢，管理部門決定解雇一些勞工。

As the company is losing a lot of money, the management has decided to l_____ o_____ some workers.

2. Brian 一走出他的辦公大樓就下起了大雨。

N_____ s_____ had Brian walked out of his office building t_____ it began to rain heavily.

3. 這把刀是用來將水果切成小塊的。

The knife i_____ u_____ t_____ cut fruits into small pieces.

4. 這些小偷在警察到達現場之前就逃走了。

The thieves g_____ a_____ before the police arrived at the scene.

5. 戶外演唱會結束之後，觀眾留下大量的垃圾在公園裡。

After the outdoor concert, the audience l_____ b_____ a great amount of trash in the park.

# Round 2

## I. Multiple Choice

(    ) 1. The blazing sun melted my ice cream, making my hands _____.

       (A) sticky       (B) rocky       (C) lively       (D) mighty

(    ) 2. The rare disease _____ Helen's immune system and made her body vulnerable.

       (A) crippled       (B) sparked       (C) guided       (D) sketched

(    ) 3. The merchant is very _____ to the needy. He often donates money to charities.

       (A) stingy       (B) random       (C) willing       (D) generous

(    ) 4. After the party, used plates and glasses were left _____ around on the table and the floor. It would take hours to clean the mess up.

       (A) slaying       (B) defying       (C) lying       (D) damming

(    ) 5. A teacher is supposed to be familiar with various kinds of teaching _____ and materials.

       (A) calculations    (B) techniques    (C) sensations    (D) forecasts

(    ) 6. To our surprise, the manager didn't give any _____ that he would like to quit the job.

       (A) ink       (B) doubt       (C) proposal       (D) hint

(    ) 7. It takes constant practice to _____ reading and writing skills.

       (A) manufacture    (B) master       (C) microwave       (D) major

(    ) 8. The boots made of genuine leather are much more expensive than those made of _____ leather.

       (A) artificial       (B) natural       (C) artistic       (D) memorable

(　　) 9. The students are so excited that they can hardly sit _____.

(A) adverse　　(B) liberal　　(C) deep　　(D) still

(　　) 10. When you enter a movie theater, be sure to know where the nearest _____ exit is.

(A) emergency　(B) embrace　(C) empire　(D) embassy

(　　) 11. It was _____ that ships and aircraft disappeared without a trace in the Bermuda Triangle.

(A) sophisticated (B) talkative　(C) inevitable　(D) mysterious

(　　) 12. I cannot stand the _____ weather there. The temperature is usually below 5°C.

(A) fair　　(B) warm　　(C) bitter　　(D) dynamic

(　　) 13. The software engineer is under great _____ because of his heavy workload.

(A) stress　(B) information　(C) investigation (D) nationality

(　　) 14. Sweet and sour pork is one of the _____ in this Chinese restaurant.

(A) slippers　(B) pumps　(C) specialties　(D) leftovers

(　　) 15. The director is known for his horror movies, but his latest one is a _____.

(A) capability　(B) comedy　(C) battery　(D) ministry

(　　) 16. Bill's academic performance in high school was good, so he won a(n) _____ to the university.

(A) background　(B) application　(C) scholarship　(D) circulation

(　　) 17. These guns and bombs are purely _____ weapons. Their firepower is not sufficient for a full-scale invasion.

(A) circular　(B) defensive　(C) ivory　(D) ambiguous

(　　) 18. Does anyone want _____ beef? I just took it out of the oven.

(A) honest　(B) roast　(C) moist　(D) vast

(     ) 19. The flight attendants standing at the entry door welcomed the passengers _____ .

    (A) abroad      (B) broad      (C) aboard      (D) board

(     ) 20. Sales of sneakers are _____ because playing sports has become an important part in people's daily lives.

    (A) spicing      (B) lacing      (C) outlining      (D) soaring

## II. Fill in the Blank （從下方選出適合字彙做適當變化，填入答案）

| distinguish | stick | dispute | burst | action |
|---|---|---|---|---|

_____ 1. Mr. and Mrs. Tyler often _____ over their children's education.

_____ 2. Tim's joke was so funny that everyone _____ out laughing.

_____ 3. I believe it's time to put the plan into _____ .

_____ 4. Claire lacks patience. She seldom _____ to anything for a long time.

_____ 5. My parents taught me how to _____ between right and wrong.

## III. Guided Translation （寫出完整字彙）

1. 不用擔心。問題遲早會解決的。

Don't worry. The problem will be solved s_____ o_____ l_____ .

2. 老兵激動地述說著他的故事，裡頭的人物似乎活靈活現起來了。

The old soldier narrated his stories so passionately that the characters seemed to c_____ t_____ l_____ .

3. 人們被鼓勵好好利用時間學習新事物。

People are encouraged to m_____ g_____ u_____ o_____ their time to learn new things.

4. 如果 Henry 想成為一名優秀的演講者，他必須得先克服對公開演說的恐懼。

If Henry wants to be a good speaker, he has to g_____

o_____ his fear of public speaking first.

5. 只要你保證車況良好，你就可以借車。

You may borrow the car a_____ l_____

a_____ you promise to keep it in good condition.

# Round 3

## I. Multiple Choice

(　　) 1. Have you seen the funny picture showing my little brother striking a dramatic _____?

    (A) image　　　　(B) pose　　　　(C) detail　　　　(D) fame

(　　) 2. The Jones' house is _____ without any furniture since they're moving into a bigger one.

    (A) frequent　　(B) bare　　　　(C) rid　　　　(D) tense

(　　) 3. Louis was a terrible traveling _____ because he was always complaining.

    (A) accent　　　(B) visa　　　　(C) companion　　(D) airline

(　　) 4. Your idea is too _____ to understand. Can you give us some concrete examples?

    (A) abstract　　(B) appropriate　(C) extinct　　(D) organized

(　　) 5. Most of the international companies will hire local _____ to give legal advice.

    (A) respondents　　　　　　(B) entrepreneurs

    (C) shareholders　　　　　　(D) attorneys

(　　) 6. I have some _____ in agreeing to the plan. I fear it may not be practical.

    (A) complaint　(B) corruption　(C) revolution　(D) hesitation

(　　) 7. The little girl is quite thoughtful and _____ compared to others of her age.

    (A) odd　　　　(B) annoying　　(C) mature　　　(D) foul

(　　) 8. Adam ought to be ＿＿＿＿ of himself for telling such a lie.

    (A) cooperative              (B) overwhelming

    (C) responsible              (D) ashamed

(　　) 9. I don't like to take part in ＿＿＿＿ activities. I am not used to facing strangers.

    (A) facial      (B) social      (C) creative      (D) reliable

(　　) 10. The author's first novel became a hit ＿＿＿＿ after it was published.

    (A) indecisively   (B) brutally     (C) instantly     (D) orally

(　　) 11. At the dinner table, you should wipe your mouth with a ＿＿＿＿ rather than with your hand.

    (A) saucer     (B) necklace     (C) stocking     (D) napkin

(　　) 12. Whenever I see a complicated math problem, my mind goes ＿＿＿＿.

    (A) blank     (B) blind     (C) wrong     (D) sour

(　　) 13. It is a(n) ＿＿＿＿ to eat mooncakes on the Moon Festival in Taiwan.

    (A) tradition     (B) invention     (C) tuition     (D) resolution

(　　) 14. The criminal showed no ＿＿＿＿ while hearing the verdict. No one knew how she felt about it.

    (A) delight     (B) emotion     (C) factor     (D) limit

(　　) 15. The rescue ＿＿＿＿ went quite smoothly. All the passengers and crew members were saved from the sinking ship in the end.

    (A) portion     (B) classification   (C) operation     (D) technology

(　　) 16. People may be fined or even jailed for illegally ＿＿＿＿ wild animals such as leopard cats and Formosan black bears.

    (A) capturing     (B) responding   (C) cooperating   (D) deploying

(　　) 17. Chloe considered it impolite to make ＿＿＿＿ when eating soup.

    (A) graphics     (B) sounds     (C) commitments (D) decisions

( 　　　 ) 18. It's a pity that the local government is too poor to _____ the research program.

(A) conquer　　　(B) compel　　　(C) finance　　　(D) download

( 　　　 ) 19. With the unemployment rate rising, a large _____ of the people in the city can't find a job.

(A) philosophy　　(B) portrait　　(C) priority　　(D) percentage

( 　　　 ) 20. An oil tanker grounded on a reef in Alaska, and millions of tons of oil was _____ into Prince William Sound.

(A) leaking　　　(B) lumping　　　(C) leaping　　　(D) layering

## II. Fill in the Blank（從下方選出適合字彙做適當變化，填入答案）

| advance | tremble | lean | cake | distribute |
|---|---|---|---|---|

_____ 1. You can always _____ on me every time you encounter problems.

_____ 2. It is a piece of _____ for the intelligent student to solve this math problem.

_____ 3. Before Zoe made a speech, she was so nervous that she couldn't stop _____.

_____ 4. On the first day of school, these textbooks will be _____ to all of the new students.

_____ 5. If you are going to go to the costume party, please let me know in _____.

## III. Guided Translation（寫出完整字彙）

1. 除了說話能力之外，人類還使用手勢來互相溝通。

I_____ a_____ t_____ speech, humans use gestures to communicate with one another.

2. 今天早上，那名怠惰的學生和往常一樣遲到了。

This morning, the lazy student was late for school a_____

u_____.

3. 老闆堅持認為，這名員工應該彌補他為公司造成的損失。

The boss insisted that the worker should m_____ u_____

f_____ the damage he had caused to the company.

4. 這電影有一些部分我不喜歡，但總體上這是一部令人愉快的電影。

There are a few parts that I don't like about the movie, but b_____

a_____ l_____ it's an enjoyable film.

5. 男孩咬住自己的嘴唇，以免自己在大眾面前哭泣。

The boy b_____ his l_____ to stop himself from crying in

public.

# Round 4

## I. Multiple Choice

(　　) 1. The _____ for drunk driving in this country can be several years' imprisonment.

    (A) objection　　(B) installation　　(C) penalty　　(D) reward

(　　) 2. A taxi can carry a _____ of four passengers. Now that there are six of us, we need two taxis.

    (A) maximum　　(B) mineral　　(C) magazine　　(D) minimum

(　　) 3. The Central Mountain Range _____ for hundreds of kilometers from north to south.

    (A) prevents　　(B) reacts　　(C) stretches　　(D) counts

(　　) 4. There is no magic _____ for success. Success belongs to those who work hard.

    (A) receipt　　(B) formula　　(C) curve　　(D) debut

(　　) 5. Many weight-conscious people have _____ meat instead of fatty meat in their meals.

    (A) slight　　(B) slender　　(C) slim　　(D) lean

(　　) 6. The TV series is an _____ reflection of lives and relationships in New York City.

    (A) accurate　　(B) efficient　　(C) official　　(D) intense

(　　) 7. What the news said is not always a fair _____ of what really happened.

    (A) instrument　　(B) statement　　(C) movement　　(D) experiment

(　　) 8. Many people screamed in _____ when they heard gunshots while watching the movie.

(A) regret　　　　　　　　　　(B) disappointment

(C) horror　　　　　　　　　　(D) amusement

(　　) 9. Maggie and her family have successfully _____ a huge ship model.

(A) assembled　　(B) assured　　(C) assumed　　(D) asserted

(　　) 10. It was regretful that the patient died of a serious infection _____ after the surgery.

(A) highly　　　(B) ordinarily　　(C) shortly　　(D) extremely

(　　) 11. Oliver lives on a below-average _____, so he can't afford luxuries.

(A) evaluation　　(B) rank　　(C) rate　　(D) income

(　　) 12. While cooking dinner, Matilda cut her finger accidentally and _____ a lot.

(A) rushed　　　(B) fled　　(C) streamed　　(D) bled

(　　) 13. The _____ economy actually benefits the environment. It helps to make better use of spare properties.

(A) sharing　　　(B) occupying　　(C) flashing　　(D) provoking

(　　) 14. My English teacher places great _____ on written work and oral practice.

(A) intonation　　(B) emphasis　　(C) guidance　　(D) dimension

(　　) 15. There will be a big sale on the online shopping website. I won't miss the _____ to pick up a few good bargains.

(A) advantage　　(B) opportunity　　(C) benefit　　(D) registration

(　　) 16. It was improper for tourists to _____ their names on the tree trunk.

(A) erase　　　(B) arrange　　(C) awe　　(D) carve

( ) 17. The actor felt _____ for the homeless children and donated some money to help them.
(A) embarrassment
(B) sympathy
(C) destiny
(D) depression

( ) 18. The driver was heavily _____ for speeding on the freeway.
(A) fined
(B) defeated
(C) crept
(D) hastened

( ) 19. This is private property. People cannot enter without _____.
(A) auction
(B) description
(C) permission
(D) procession

( ) 20. The artist is _____ with creative talents. His original works impress all those who have been to his exhibitions.
(A) visible
(B) doubtful
(C) faithful
(D) gifted

## II. Fill in the Blank （從下方選出適合字彙做適當變化，填入答案）

| length | draw | vain | advantage | starve |
| --- | --- | --- | --- | --- |

_____ 1. Our efforts were in _____ because none of the methods worked.

_____ 2. Some people go to great _____ to stay in perfect shape.

_____ 3. I'm _____. Let's go to the snack bar and get something to eat.

_____ 4. The hostess is _____ up a list of the guests for the tea party.

_____ 5. We should take _____ of the department store's annual sale and buy some clothes.

## III. Guided Translation （寫出完整字彙）

1. 你最好聽從你父親的建議。他經驗比你豐富。

   You had better l_____ t_____ your father's advice. He has more experience than you.

2. 你能檢查是否有足夠的蘋果以滿足需求嗎？客人要來了！

   Would you please check if there are enough apples to g_____ a_____? The guests are coming!

3. 不下一百名公車司機罷工，抗議他們的低工資和長工時。

   There were n_____ l_____ t_____ a hundred bus drivers going on strike in protest over their low wages and long working hours.

4. 像那位店主如此不誠實的人肯定會失敗。

   Such a dishonest man as the shopkeeper i_____ s_____ t_____ fail.

5. Howard 不喜歡打高爾夫球。他覺得很無聊。

   Howard doesn't g_____ i_____ f_____ golf. He finds it very boring.

# Round 5

## I. Multiple Choice

(　　) 1. I think this product best fulfills my _____. Therefore, I will buy it.
　　　　(A) requirements　(B) monuments　(C) agreements　(D) documents

(　　) 2. The castle is _____ by trees. Everything we see from the window is green.
　　　　(A) threatened　(B) wrapped　(C) surrounded　(D) astonished

(　　) 3. The patient is receiving new _____ for lung cancer at the moment.
　　　　(A) aggression　(B) chart　(C) carriage　(D) treatment

(　　) 4. Ms. Spencer is going to give a _____ on business management next week.
　　　　(A) lettuce　(B) lecture　(C) gesture　(D) miniature

(　　) 5. The entrepreneur has a lot of business _____ but very few real friends.
　　　　(A) prisoners
　　　　(C) immigrants
　　　　(B) ministers
　　　　(D) acquaintances

(　　) 6. The politician filed a _____ against the hater that spread rumors on the Internet.
　　　　(A) discourse　(B) constraint　(C) lawsuit　(D) verdict

(　　) 7. Chris _____ his bedroom before he bought a bed and a bookshelf.
　　　　(A) lengthened　(B) blended　(C) researched　(D) measured

(　　) 8. The French restaurant that offers excellent food and has a romantic _____ is very popular with couples.
　　　　(A) atmosphere
　　　　(C) square
　　　　(B) specialty
　　　　(D) recommendation

( ) 9. The refugees are badly in need of _____. They lack clothing and food.
(A) supervisors　(B) surfaces　(C) supplies　(D) superstitions

( ) 10. There is every _____ that the cancer patient will recover soon.
(A) independence (B) individual　(C) indication　(D) illusion

( ) 11. At the international conference, you can meet people of different _____.
(A) dilemmas　(B) nationalities　(C) authorities　(D) humanities

( ) 12. Olivia is my best friend. I often share my _____ and joys with her.
(A) pillows　(B) hollows　(C) flows　(D) sorrows

( ) 13. I don't think you can justify the _____ of child labor. That's illegal!
(A) removal　(B) employment　(C) invasion　(D) dismissal

( ) 14. You have the right to assert yourself, but at the same time, you should listen to the _____ point of view.
(A) opposite　(B) classical　(C) troublesome　(D) excessive

( ) 15. For some people, _____ clothes mean a T-shirt and jeans.
(A) casual　(B) acid　(C) fit　(D) spiritual

( ) 16. Leo's roommate is such an ill-mannered fellow. How can Leo _____ his rudeness?
(A) express　(B) demonstrate　(C) tolerate　(D) exchange

( ) 17. The airplane burst into _____, and all the passengers were killed immediately.
(A) wagons　(B) flames　(C) tears　(D) flashes

( ) 18. No matter how hard Julie tried, she still couldn't _____ her boss to accept the proposal.
(A) persuade　(B) demand　(C) refund　(D) compose

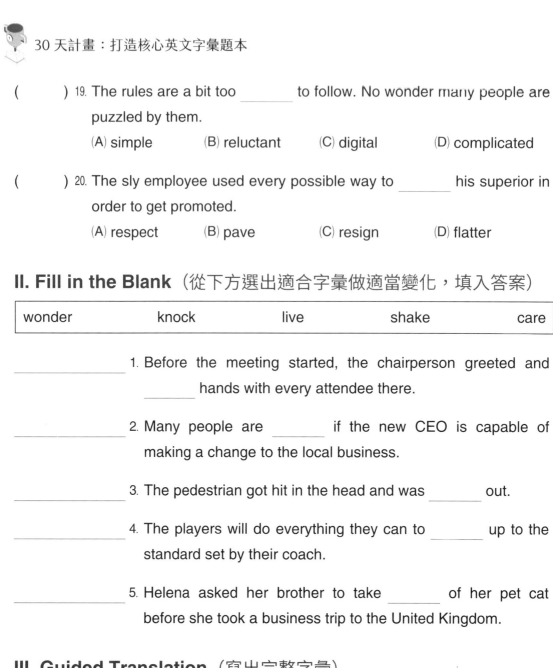

(     ) 19. The rules are a bit too _____ to follow. No wonder many people are puzzled by them.

(A) simple      (B) reluctant      (C) digital      (D) complicated

(     ) 20. The sly employee used every possible way to _____ his superior in order to get promoted.

(A) respect      (B) pave      (C) resign      (D) flatter

## II. Fill in the Blank （從下方選出適合字彙做適當變化，填入答案）

| wonder | knock | live | shake | care |
| --- | --- | --- | --- | --- |

_____ 1. Before the meeting started, the chairperson greeted and _____ hands with every attendee there.

_____ 2. Many people are _____ if the new CEO is capable of making a change to the local business.

_____ 3. The pedestrian got hit in the head and was _____ out.

_____ 4. The players will do everything they can to _____ up to the standard set by their coach.

_____ 5. Helena asked her brother to take _____ of her pet cat before she took a business trip to the United Kingdom.

## III. Guided Translation （寫出完整字彙）

1. Frank 害怕如果他入學考試不及格，會讓他的父母失望。

Frank is afraid that if he fails the entrance exam, he may l_____ his parents d_____.

2. 新款的護膚產品去年帶來一千萬的收入。

The new skin-care product b_____ i_____ ten million dollars last year.

3. 這場音樂會已被延後到下個月。

The concert has been p_____ o_____ until next month.

4. Susan 開去加油站，因為她快沒油了。

Susan drove to the gas station because she almost r_____ o_____ o_____ gas.

5. 現在沒有必要討論細節了。我需要的是文章的主旨。

There is no need to g_____ i_____ details now. What I need is the main idea of the article.

# Round 6

## I. Multiple Choice

(　　) 1. When my colleague Betty called me a workaholic, I took it as a _____.

    (A) compensation (B) composition　(C) component　(D) compliment

(　　) 2. The missing boy was found _____ the streets alone this afternoon.

    (A) wondering　(B) winding　(C) wrecking　(D) wandering

(　　) 3. The bad news came as a great _____ to me. I cannot believe it at all.

    (A) shock　　　　　　　(B) resistance

    (C) demonstration　　　　(D) accomplishment

(　　) 4. In winter, the surface of the lake _____, and people had fun going skating on it.

    (A) sought　(B) frightened　(C) abused　(D) froze

(　　) 5. A will is a type of _____ document concerning how property or money should be handled after someone dies.

    (A) gentle　(B) legal　(C) colonial　(D) foggy

(　　) 6. The singer _____ the smoking habit at 15 and is trying his best to quit it now.

    (A) acquired　(B) required　(C) tickled　(D) enclosed

(　　) 7. Li Bai, who was known as "the God of Poetry" in China, was a poet _____ of the name.

    (A) worthy　(B) jealous　(C) fond　(D) considerate

( ) 8. The increasing popularity of electric cars is expected to reduce vehicle _____.

(A) emissions     (B) vouchers     (C) syndromes     (D) predators

( ) 9. Jessica had difficulty _____ her PIN number, so she downloaded a note-taking app to remind herself of it.

(A) yelling     (B) managing     (C) memorizing     (D) slipping

( ) 10. The job candidate was asked to _____ his photo to the application form.

(A) accuse     (B) collect     (C) attach     (D) grip

( ) 11. Many animals would _____ food and go into deep sleep to get through the winter.

(A) store     (B) stir     (C) strike     (D) struggle

( ) 12. Jack's survival _____ told him to lie still and pretend to be dead.

(A) attic     (B) instinct     (C) revenue     (D) density

( ) 13. Nancy speaks French so fluently that she sounds exactly like a _____ speaker.

(A) national     (B) native     (C) local     (D) weird

( ) 14. There's something in your right eye — try _____ your eyes a few times.

(A) covering     (B) heeling     (C) craning     (D) blinking

( ) 15. In Western culture, both black cats and the number thirteen are considered to be _____ of bad luck.

(A) limbs     (B) doses     (C) symbols     (D) agendas

( ) 16. Everyone has to do something to keep _____ species from dying out.

(A) exclusive     (B) endangered     (C) elegant     (D) enormous

( ) 17. These grapes imported from Japan have a special smell and taste that is different from _____ ones.
(A) unique (B) talented (C) ideal (D) ordinary

( ) 18. During the strike, the management expressed the desire to enter into direct _____ with the employees.
(A) entrance (B) catalogue (C) dialogue (D) cooperation

( ) 19. The _____ of the candidate's election campaign is "Trust me with your future."
(A) eraser (B) theme (C) slogan (D) headline

( ) 20. Jennie gave me a _____ refusal, which made me feel discouraged.
(A) faint (B) flat (C) fake (D) fine

## II. Fill in the Blank (從下方選出適合字彙做適當變化，填入答案)

| catch | divorce | leave | shape | shame |
|-------|---------|-------|-------|-------|

_____ 1. The nasty remarks that the politician had made on the TV show brought _____ on his political party.

_____ 2. The husband _____ his wife behind and never came back to her again.

_____ 3. Will printed dresses _____ on as the most fashionable clothes again?

_____ 4. To attract the attention of children, the baker made the cookies in the _____ of animals.

_____ 5. Most fans just want to see the best athletes competing for the love of sports and believe sports should be _____ from politics.

## III. Guided Translation（寫出完整字彙）

1. 既然日子很苦，我們必須擺脫奢侈。

   Since times are very hard, we have to d_____ a_____
   w_____ luxuries.

2. 我成功的秘訣在於勤奮和毅力。

   The secret of my success l_____ i_____ diligence and
   perseverance.

3. Victoria 討厭搭飛機旅行，因為她經常暈機。

   Victoria hates traveling b_____ a_____ because she
   often gets airsick.

4. 這對雙胞胎長得太像了，我分不清誰是誰。

   The twins look so alike that I cannot t_____ one f_____
   the other.

5. 令人們失望的是，總統沒有信守他的諾言。

   To the people's disappointment, the president didn't k_____ his
   p_____.

# Round 7

## I. Multiple Choice

(　　) 1. Timothy was so shy that he ＿＿＿ while delivering a speech in front of the whole class.
(A) focused　　(B) blushed　　(C) slid　　(D) trapped

(　　) 2. Daphne is a ＿＿＿ person. She can adapt to new surroundings easily.
(A) flexible　　(B) persuasive　　(C) graceful　　(D) tropical

(　　) 3. The magician waved his magic wand over the rabbit and made it ＿＿＿.
(A) visit　　(B) value　　(C) vanish　　(D) view

(　　) 4. The hospital was ＿＿＿ in 1920. It has been serving patients since then.
(A) founded　　(B) folded　　(C) flamed　　(D) fanned

(　　) 5. The merchant cannot guarantee ＿＿＿ supplies of rubbing alcohol and face masks because the demands are high.
(A) contagious　　(B) effective　　(C) adequate　　(D) alternative

(　　) 6. The border dispute between the two countries has created a tense ＿＿＿.
(A) significance　　(B) situation　　(C) signature　　(D) sincerity

(　　) 7. It was a great honor for the soldier to receive special ＿＿＿ from the president during his speech.
(A) effort　　(B) relation　　(C) use　　(D) mention

( ) 8. None of the political refugees' _____ to contact the outside world was successful.

(A) warnings     (B) trials     (C) remedies     (D) attempts

( ) 9. Buses or MRT are my mother's means of _____ to work.

(A) transportation         (B) admiration

(C) digestion         (D) concentration

( ) 10. Gina was late for work this morning because she was stuck in a traffic _____ for an hour.

(A) jewel     (B) jelly     (C) jaw     (D) jam

( ) 11. The manager is so _____. It is impossible for him to change his mind.

(A) glorious     (B) stubborn     (C) diligent     (D) energetic

( ) 12. We all wish for _____ peace in the world and that no country would fight another country.

(A) practical     (B) enduring     (C) internal     (D) domestic

( ) 13. If an apple is grown _____, that means the farmer does not use chemical fertilizer on it.

(A) organically     (B) biologically     (C) economically     (D) effectively

( ) 14. To save marine life, people must _____ dumping trash into the sea.

(A) permit     (B) protect     (C) practice     (D) cease

( ) 15. Before the vehicles powered by electricity were invented, people mainly used _____ as power.

(A) fulfillment     (B) prosperity     (C) gasoline     (D) recovery

( ) 16. The _____ gave Mr. Williams a check-up and told him everything was normal.

(A) photographer     (B) philosopher     (C) physicist     (D) physician

( ) 17. The _____ of global village is now widely accepted by the public.

(A) concern     (B) concept     (C) equality     (D) analysis

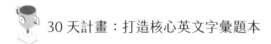

( ) 18. The pilot's miraculous survival after the plane crash has become a
_____ . It is still remembered and talked about even after ten years.
(A) burglar (B) peanut (C) legend (D) socket

( ) 19. Holding his baby in his arms, the father _____ a lullaby to her in a
soft voice.
(A) hugged (B) hammered (C) hummed (D) hushed

( ) 20. The scenic attraction was _____ by a large number of tourists
during the long vacation.
(A) invaded (B) prayed (C) restored (D) investigated

## II. Fill in the Blank （從下方選出適合字彙做適當變化，填入答案）

| afford | panic | transfer | question | shelter |
| --- | --- | --- | --- | --- |

_____ 1. The family can't _____ daily necessities, let alone a piece
of real estate.

_____ 2. Even though the hiker was lost in the forest, he didn't get into
a(n) _____ and managed to find a way out.

_____ 3. The passers-by took _____ in the doorway because of the
downpour.

_____ 4. The Watson family can hardly make ends meet, so it is out of
the _____ for them to go on vacation.

_____ 5. Emily was _____ from the headquarter to the branch in
Paris along with three other engineers.

## III. Guided Translation （寫出完整字彙）

1. 行人過馬路時必須注意來往的車輛。
Pedestrians have to l_____ o_____ for the passing cars
when crossing the road.

2. 放下你的漫畫書，馬上做作業。

P_____ your comic book d_____ and do your homework right now.

3. 這個協定只有一年有效，而明年應該續簽。

This agreement is only v_____ f_____ a year, and it should be renewed next year.

4. 你最好帶上羽絨衣以防半夜山上下雪。

You had better take the down coat with you i_____ c_____ it snows in the mountains at midnight.

5. 這對夫妻經歷了婚姻的風風雨雨。

The couple has made it through the u_____ and d_____ of their marriage.

# Round 8

## I. Multiple Choice

(      ) 1. The plumber _____ the screw by turning it counterclockwise.
       (A) labored      (B) lengthened      (C) loosened      (D) flooded

(      ) 2. The economic depression has led to many small businesses' _____.
       (A) steadiness      (B) attachment      (C) blindness      (D) bankruptcy

(      ) 3. Playing sports has many advantages. For example, it helps you build up your physical _____.
       (A) humidity      (B) strength      (C) faith      (D) explosion

(      ) 4. In Chinese culture, it is very improper for people to attend a _____ in red or other bright colors.
       (A) funeral      (B) launch      (C) church      (D) wedding

(      ) 5. After a tiring day, it is relaxing to take a _____ walk along the beach.
       (A) leisurely      (B) deadly      (C) silly      (D) costly

(      ) 6. The political party has tended to _____ more moderate policies these years.
       (A) adapt      (B) adjust      (C) adopt      (D) advise

(      ) 7. The nurse felt _____ and yawned after a 12-hour shift.
       (A) asleep      (B) awake      (C) sleepy      (D) lousy

(      ) 8. I think every member of a family should help with the _____ chores.
       (A) psychological (B) household      (C) eventual      (D) immediate

(      ) 9. The prisoner of war begged his enemy for _____ when pointed with a gun.
       (A) acceptance      (B) mercy      (C) assistance      (D) blouse

( ) 10. Having a positive _____ toward life, Bill can cope with stressful situations in a healthy way.

(A) jealousy     (B) interruption     (C) preference     (D) attitude

( ) 11. Paula shrugged her _____ and said she had no idea about the plan.

(A) fists     (B) palms     (C) necks     (D) shoulders

( ) 12. The smartphone is no longer a fancy modern device. It has become a(n) _____ for many people.

(A) necessity     (B) lobster     (C) array     (D) orientation

( ) 13. Some parents take pleasure in _____ about their children's remarkable achievements.

(A) boasting     (B) teasing     (C) complaining     (D) complying

( ) 14. Matilda _____ the pearl necklace that her beloved grandmother left her after her death.

(A) determined     (B) regulated     (C) wasted     (D) treasured

( ) 15. If the classroom discipline isn't properly _____, there will be chaos.

(A) giggled     (B) afforded     (C) enforced     (D) proceeded

( ) 16. The United Nations is a(n) _____ meant to promote international cooperation and world peace.

(A) accommodation     (B) organization

(C) occasion     (D) petition

( ) 17. The foldable smartphone is only 8 _____ long when folded.

(A) meters     (B) kilometers     (C) centimeters     (D) feet

( ) 18. All the _____ and field events are going to be very competitive and challenging.

(A) track     (B) distance     (C) option     (D) weight

(    ) 19. Many people do not realize that downloading videos or music online without permission would constitute _____.

(A) processing     (B) collecting     (C) pirating     (D) notifying

(    ) 20. I'd like to _____ my reservation for a single room on August 12.

(A) confess     (B) confirm     (C) conclude     (D) commute

## II. Fill in the Blank （從下方選出適合字彙做適當變化，填入答案）

| amount | picture | shine | center | effort |
| --- | --- | --- | --- | --- |

_____ 1. No matter how hard the witness tried to explain, the police still couldn't get the _____ of the whole situation.

_____ 2. Put the vase in the _____ of the table so that it won't be knocked off.

_____ 3. Rain or _____, mail carriers deliver mail regularly every day.

_____ 4. Miley spares no _____ in helping the homeless children.

_____ 5. According to the news report, the number of the flood victims has _____ to twenty.

## III. Guided Translation （寫出完整字彙）

1. 請把電視的音量調小。我現在需要一個安靜的地方念書。

Please t_____ d_____ the volume of the TV set. I need a quiet place to study now.

2. 渡輪被海面上的濃霧所阻。

The ferryboat was h_____ u_____ by a thick blanket of fog on the sea.

3. 這個地方改變太多以至於我們混淆且找不到路了。

The place had changed so much that we got m_____ u_____ and couldn't find our way.

4. 從臺北飛往紐約市的航程需要 16 個小時左右。

The flight from Taipei to New York City takes sixteen hours o_____

s_____.

5. 請稍等一下。經理正在接另一通電話。

H_____ o_____ a minute, please. The manager is on the other line right now.

# Round 9

## I. Multiple Choice

(     ) 1. Coupons and discounts create an _____ for shoppers to purchase more items in a supermarket.

     (A) intensity     (B) interaction     (C) incentive     (D) initiative

(     ) 2. The complaints from the citizens are too _____ to ignore, so the government has to take action to solve the problem.

     (A) junior     (B) spacious     (C) numerous     (D) curious

(     ) 3. A new skyscraper is going to be built on the _____ next year.

     (A) site     (B) viewpoint     (C) development   (D) elevator

(     ) 4. The car is gradually _____ speed. It is going faster and faster.

     (A) reducing     (B) gathering     (C) preparing     (D) reaching

(     ) 5. A(n) _____ society should be tolerant and allow the existence of different ideas and beliefs.

     (A) administrative            (B) radical

     (C) traditional              (D) liberal

(     ) 6. It is _____ for you to look for some information about the company online before you go for the job interview.

     (A) adventurous           (B) advantageous

     (C) prompt                (D) abundant

(     ) 7. The wooden bridge is too weak to _____ the heavy truck.

     (A) surrender     (B) support     (C) confine     (D) drag

(     ) 8. The psychologist is currently doing research on _____ behavior.

     (A) hollow     (B) human     (C) hourly     (D) horizontal

(     ) 9. One of the _____ of living with your parents is that you don't have to pay the rent.
    (A) disadvantages               (B) stances
    (C) merits                      (D) characters

(     ) 10. The famous scientist gave speeches to _____ all over the world.
    (A) markers      (B) siblings      (C) semesters      (D) audiences

(     ) 11. The delivery rider was caught in the heavy rain and got _____ to the skin.
    (A) idle      (B) vague      (C) passive      (D) soaked

(     ) 12. Most people believe that the criminal will be brought to _____ sooner or later.
    (A) prejudice      (B) junk      (C) injury      (D) justice

(     ) 13. The employees were disappointed that the boss gave a _____ answer to their request for a pay raise.
    (A) universal      (B) countless      (C) negative      (D) grave

(     ) 14. English has _____ many words from French and German.
    (A) borrowed      (B) lent      (C) discovered      (D) invented

(     ) 15. The hunter _____ at the deer with his rifle, but he missed it.
    (A) shaved      (B) shot      (C) shifted      (D) shook

(     ) 16. Tommy felt a pang of _____ when he saw his brother get a new bike as a birthday gift.
    (A) tendency      (B) fantasy      (C) property      (D) envy

(     ) 17. The attorney is a _____ person. Even her books are arranged in alphabetical order.
    (A) well-organized           (B) well-educated
    (C) well-behaved            (D) well-informed

( ) 18. I don't think I can continue doing the job. It's extremely _____ for me.

(A) challenging (B) automatic (C) proper (D) loose

( ) 19. Maggie cut the vitamin tablet in half because it was too big for her to _____.

(A) spit (B) screw (C) swallow (D) swear

( ) 20. After the presidential election, there _____ months of conflicts within the political party.

(A) followed (B) funded (C) filtered (D) fastened

## II. Fill in the Blank（從下方選出適合字彙做適當變化，填入答案）

| certain | acquaintance | suppose | chance | furious |
| --- | --- | --- | --- | --- |

_____ 1. Even if both sides agree to cease fire, how can they make _____ neither of them will break the agreement again?

_____ 2. I don't know much about the author. I only have a nodding _____ with his books.

_____ 3. Kevin's parents were _____ with him, for he came home very late last night.

_____ 4. Owing to the possible damage caused by the approaching typhoon, we are _____ to make some preparations in advance.

_____ 5. Doris got the job completely by _____. She happened to be the only applicant.

## III. Guided Translation（寫出完整字彙）

1. 二十年前，這個國家的人民很窮，主要以番薯維生。

Twenty years ago, people in this country were very poor and l_____ mainly o_____ yams.

2. Cynthia 是如此善良且富同情心。如果我處在她的位置,我不會給她懶惰的弟弟任何錢。

   Cynthia is so kind and sympathetic. If I were i＿＿＿＿＿＿ her s＿＿＿＿＿＿, I would not give her lazy brother any money.

3. 這對夫妻決定停止爭吵,並互相談和。

   The couple decided to stop fighting and m＿＿＿＿＿＿ p＿＿＿＿＿＿ with each other.

4. John 和我輪流開車,所以我們都可以休息一下。

   John and I t＿＿＿＿＿＿ t＿＿＿＿＿＿ driving, so both of us could get some rest.

5. 面對難纏的顧客,接待員努力強忍著怒火。

   Dealing with the difficult customer, the receptionist tried hard to h＿＿＿＿＿＿ b＿＿＿＿＿＿ his anger.

# Round 10

## I. Multiple Choice

(     ) 1. I don't want to miss the _____ music festival. After all, it is held only once a year.
    (A) private      (B) annual      (C) moral      (D) subtle

(     ) 2. Pete could just see the path ahead in the weak _____ of a flashlight.
    (A) bean      (B) bead      (C) beam      (D) battle

(     ) 3. It is not easy for an untrained hiker to scramble up such a _____ cliff.
    (A) steep      (B) steady      (C) stable      (D) standard

(     ) 4. The tourists raised their heads and _____ at the bright stars in astonishment.
    (A) glimpsed      (B) glared      (C) gazed      (D) grabbed

(     ) 5. Some people in a democratic country may not understand the true meaning of _____ and tend to abuse it.
    (A) education      (B) liberty      (C) affection      (D) ability

(     ) 6. The performance of the visiting team was _____ by the hot weather, so they lost the game.
    (A) reduced      (B) injured      (C) adored      (D) affected

(     ) 7. A headache, a sore throat, fatigue, and muscle aches are all _____ symptoms of the flu.
    (A) minor      (B) naked      (C) typical      (D) bizarre

(     ) 8. The inflation rate has reached a(n) _____ level because of the war.
    (A) cognitive                  (B) sustainable
    (C) imaginative              (D) unprecedented

(   ) 9. Bob is not _____ at present. Should I ask him to call you back?

    (A) affordable     (B) consecutive    (C) collective     (D) available

(   ) 10. Jessica worked as a YouTuber before _____ to the entertainment industry.

    (A) switching     (B) sweeping     (C) stitching     (D) supposing

(   ) 11. The little boy fell off his bike, and his trousers were torn at the _____.

    (A) elbows      (B) arms       (C) knees       (D) thumbs

(   ) 12. The parents were accused of _____ their children because they failed to provide them with proper food and care.

    (A) dominating    (B) tolerating     (C) spoiling      (D) neglecting

(   ) 13. On weekends, it is common to see shoppers bargain with the _____ in the flea market.

    (A) operators     (B) vendors      (C) traitors      (D) thrillers

(   ) 14. The news came from a reliable _____. It should be accurate.

    (A) source      (B) rhythm      (C) institute     (D) verse

(   ) 15. The technician's job is to _____ how a new material stands up to wear and tear.

    (A) evaluate     (B) recycle      (C) promise     (D) constitute

(   ) 16. The stylish restaurant on the bank of the river was _____ a boathouse.

    (A) originally     (B) abnormally    (C) harmfully     (D) intensively

(   ) 17. The icy road was so _____ that we could hardly stand still.

    (A) solid       (B) slippery     (C) stale       (D) salty

(   ) 18. Because of conflicting ideologies, abortion is a(n) _____ topic in many countries.

    (A) grassy      (B) controversial   (C) oval       (D) incredible

(      ) 19. The train departs from _____ 4 at three o'clock sharp.

      (A) Stage       (B) Board       (C) Platform       (D) Panel

(      ) 20. The big fire has caused _____ damage to the historic building.

      (A) constructive       (B) constant       (C) continuous       (D) considerable

## II. Fill in the Blank （從下方選出適合字彙做適當變化，填入答案）

| mistake | doubt | appreciation | compromise | burst |
|---------|-------|--------------|------------|-------|

_____ 1. The foreign tourist got on a wrong bus by _____, which took him farther away from his destination.

_____ 2. A political refugee made a video in _____ of the help of the United Nations.

_____ 3. Lost and not knowing what to do, Amy _____ into tears at the train station.

_____ 4. After a long talk, Allen and his wife finally reached a(n) _____ over the housework issue.

_____ 5. William Shakespeare, who created many great plays and poems, was beyond _____ one of the most influential writers in the English language.

## III. Guided Translation （寫出完整字彙）

1. 在產前派對上，準媽媽收到了一份 24 小時免費保姆的禮物。

In the b_____ s_____, the mother-to-be received a gift of 24-hour free babysitting.

2. 嚴重乾旱時，這座老舊城鎮所有的水井都乾涸了。

During the severe drought, all the wells in the old town d_____ u_____.

3. 不要客氣，自己吃點披薩和汽水。

Make yourself at home and h_____ yourself t_____ some pizza and soda pop.

4. 當你和新朋友聊天時，找到有趣的話題來延續對話是很重要的。

When you c_____ w_____ a new friend, it is important to find interesting topics to keep up the conversation.

5. 你相信一見鍾情嗎？我不相信，因為第一印象可能具有欺騙性。

Do you believe in love a_____ f_____ s_____?

I don't buy it because first impressions can be deceiving.

# Round 11

## I. Multiple Choice

(　　) 1. The reason for _____ the workers with robots is to cut the cost of production.
   (A) scattering　(B) replacing　(C) offending　(D) removing

(　　) 2. The father rocked the _____ gently to calm his crying baby down.
   (A) crack　(B) crane　(C) crayon　(D) cradle

(　　) 3. The biography stated that Mozart showed _____ musical talent at the age of three.
   (A) eternal　(B) exceptional　(C) suspect　(D) harmful

(　　) 4. Environmentalists are against electricity _____ from nuclear power.
   (A) misery　(B) maturity　(C) generation　(D) shortage

(　　) 5. A bolt of _____ struck the cabin and started a fire.
   (A) blade　(B) chemistry　(C) lightning　(D) slope

(　　) 6. The dog is very _____. It barks furiously at every passerby.
   (A) extensive　(B) aggressive　(C) agreeable　(D) admirable

(　　) 7. This electronics company has a _____ of 485 full-time employees.
   (A) stuff　(B) stove　(C) straw　(D) staff

(　　) 8. Some parrots are capable of _____ human speech.
   (A) interpreting　(B) allocating　(C) imitating　(D) integrating

(　　) 9. The doctor is examining the blood cells under the _____.
   (A) microscope　(B) microwave　(C) telegraph　(D) telescope

( ) 10. The religious leader was _____ the Nobel Peace Prize for his significant contribution to world peace.

(A) competed　　(B) maintained　　(C) awarded　　(D) awoken

( ) 11. The teacher _____ a notice about the classroom rules on the board at the back of the classroom.

(A) drifted　　(B) crept　　(C) stuck　　(D) stung

( ) 12. The branch manager had to _____ with the workers so that the strike would end as soon as possible.

(A) negotiate　　(B) skate　　(C) mix　　(D) struggle

( ) 13. The tennis player kept _____ the ball against the wall.

(A) bouncing　　(B) bumping　　(C) bruising　　(D) blessing

( ) 14. Remember to stick a _____ on the envelope before you mail it.

(A) faucet　　(B) knot　　(C) harbor　　(D) stamp

( ) 15. At a rough _____, I will get the work done by next Tuesday.

(A) merchant　　(B) diagnosis　　(C) mortgage　　(D) estimate

( ) 16. There is a scratch on the driver's side, but _____, the car is in perfect condition.

(A) however　　(B) therefore　　(C) moreover　　(D) otherwise

( ) 17. Belinda is the first Olympic tennis _____ in my country.

(A) province　　(B) champion　　(C) tournament　　(D) jury

( ) 18. Having an allergy to pollen, Rachel _____ whenever she goes to her grandmother's garden.

(A) sniffs　　(B) teases　　(C) whispers　　(D) tutors

( ) 19. At the staff meeting, the boss _____ that there would be no annual bonus because of the economic depression.

(A) interrupted　　(B) announced　　(C) exploded　　(D) forgave

(     ) 20. The talk show host's sense of humor has won him great _____ across the country.

    (A) popularity     (B) population     (C) pollution     (D) position

## II. Fill in the Blank（從下方選出適合字彙做適當變化，填入答案）

| kind | similar | matter | butterfly | moment |
|------|---------|--------|-----------|--------|

_____ 1. As nobody has come to claim the stolen car, the police have to keep it for the _____.

_____ 2. Oscar had _____ in his stomach before he went for a ride on the roller coaster.

_____ 3. The Earth is _____ to an orange in shape.

_____ 4. Ivan was _____ of nervous when inviting his crush to his birthday party.

_____ 5. No _____ what obstacle lies ahead, we will not give up.

## III. Guided Translation（寫出完整字彙）

1. 如此微薄的收入，單親家庭真的很難維持生計。

With such meager earnings, it's really hard for single-parent families to m_____ b_____ e_____ m_____.

2. 不要把玩具火車拆開，因為我不知道怎麼把它裝回去。

Don't t_____ the toy train a_____ because I don't know how to put it back together.

3. Bill 丟掉他壞掉的筆電，買了一台新的。

Bill t_____ a_____ his broken laptop and bought a new one.

4. 我在工作上有任何能幫你的嗎？

   Can I be o_____ a_____ h_____ to you in the work?

5. Pamela 喜歡在傍晚和她的丈夫挽著手沿著河岸散步。

   Pamela enjoys walking a_____ i_____ a_____ with her husband along the riverbank in the evening.

# Round 12

## I. Multiple Choice

(      ) 1. We decided to _____ the meeting until the manager is back from his vacation.

       (A) postpone     (B) frame     (C) delete     (D) sacrifice

(      ) 2. With the rapid development of modern technology, it is really hard to _____ what life will be like 50 years later.

       (A) prefer     (B) present     (C) pretend     (D) predict

(      ) 3. According to the _____ to the accident, that speeding car crashed into the train.

       (A) manufacturer  (B) civilian     (C) scientist     (D) witness

(      ) 4. As the effect of _____ warming is getting more and more serious, everyone should make an effort to reduce his or her carbon footprint.

       (A) electric     (B) global     (C) heated     (D) powerful

(      ) 5. The first step of making the dish is to cook the vegetables until all the _____ is absorbed into the vegetables.

       (A) quantity     (B) solid     (C) liquid     (D) foundation

(      ) 6. It is reported that the actor is having a(n) _____ with a married woman.

       (A) affair     (B) civilization  (C) craft     (D) imagination

(      ) 7. This north part of the lake is quite _____. The boat may touch its bottom.

       (A) gigantic     (B) accessible  (C) vocal     (D) shallow

( ) 8. Your _____ of the law will one day cause you troubles.

(A) involvement    (B) innocence    (C) ignorance    (D) improvement

( ) 9. I hate being the first one to arrive at the party—it makes me feel

_____ .

(A) awkward    (B) bloody    (C) tame    (D) atomic

( ) 10. Seeing a(n) _____ seat near the door, the passenger rushed to sit there.

(A) fertile    (B) vacant    (C) abnormal    (D) hasty

( ) 11. The political leader claims that it is reasonable to enforce strict _____ in the country.

(A) discipline    (B) consequence (C) cuisine    (D) weapon

( ) 12. Sylvia lives in an unsafe _____ where many pickpockets and drug traffickers exist.

(A) precaution          (B) assignment

(C) neighborhood      (D) geography

( ) 13. After the party, Wendy decided to go home by taxi. Although the host offered her a ride, she didn't want to give him any extra _____ .

(A) buy    (B) bother    (C) scare    (D) need

( ) 14. Frank thinks that children are the poor _____ of their parents' divorce.

(A) accountants (B) critics    (C) victims    (D) applicants

( ) 15. With the _____ of the plane being delayed for an hour, it was a perfect trip.

(A) reputation    (B) exception    (C) expectation (D) reception

( ) 16. The _____ of the election won't be certain until the last vote has been counted.

(A) outline    (B) outlet    (C) outfit    (D) outcome

( ) 17. The man who was _____ with two counts of murder has been sentenced to twenty years in prison.

(A) bargained    (B) defied    (C) requested    (D) charged

( ) 18. Drivers who _____ traffic rules should be punished for their misbehavior.

(A) violate    (B) mislead    (C) obey    (D) license

( ) 19. Aaron turned to Joan for advice because she is a _____ of information on interior design.

(A) follower    (B) fountain    (C) fortune    (D) formation

( ) 20. There is still a certain percentage of the world's _____ suffering from lack of adequate nutrition.

(A) category    (B) species    (C) population    (D) settlement

## II. Fill in the Blank （從下方選出適合字彙做適當變化，填入答案）

| arrest | seat | mention | earnest | while |
|---|---|---|---|---|

_____ 1. I don't think you can lose any weight if you exercise once in a(n) _____.

_____ 2. We started to have dinner after all the guests _____ themselves.

_____ 3. The notice says that the on-the-job training will begin in _____ on June 1.

_____ 4. Christine is one of the most innovative, intelligent, not to _____ talented, candidates I've ever interviewed.

_____ 5. The robber was stopped outside the bank and put under _____.

## III. Guided Translation（寫出完整字彙）

1. 樓下的噪音把 John 從午睡中驚醒。

   The noise downstairs w_____ John u_____ from his nap.

2. 請坐，讓自己像在家一樣別拘束。

   Please   have   a   seat   and   m_____   y_____
   a_____ h_____.

3. 看到這隻可憐的小狗獨自在街上時，我別無選擇只好把牠帶回家。

   When   I   saw   the   poor   little   puppy   on   the   street,   I   h_____
   n_____   c_____   b_____   t_____
   take it home.

4. 各行各業的人都喜歡這部電視劇。它很受大家歡迎。

   People   from   a_____   w_____   o_____
   l_____ enjoy this TV series. It is very popular with everyone.

5. 這名 YouTuber 已經迷上了環遊世界的想法，她打算沿途拍攝一系列影片。

   The  YouTuber  has  g_____  h_____  o_____
   the idea of traveling around the world, and she plans to film a series of videos
   along the way.

# Round 13

## I. Multiple Choice

(　　) 1. It's common for people to use camera apps or photo editors to _____ skin imperfections nowadays.
      (A) freeze      (B) segment      (C) protest      (D) disguise

(　　) 2. It's raining outside. Why don't we have pizza _____ for dinner tonight?
      (A) resolved      (B) depressed      (C) uncovered      (D) delivered

(　　) 3. Do you know how many points a touchdown _____?
      (A) scouts      (B) scolds      (C) scores      (D) scrubs

(　　) 4. The nursery rhymes created by Mother Goose are in the public _____ in several countries.
      (A) mandate      (B) domain      (C) theology      (D) entity

(　　) 5. In many states of the United States, it is illegal to sell _____ to people under 21.
      (A) metal      (B) electricity      (C) tuna      (D) liquor

(　　) 6. Three enemy _____ have been shot down over the borderline.
      (A) vessels      (B) cruises      (C) aircrafts      (D) trains

(　　) 7. Even when times get _____, the professional athlete still works hard to practice and never gives up.
      (A) tough      (B) urban      (C) thick      (D) separate

(　　) 8. More and more people hope to _____ into a country where there are far fewer political disputes.
      (A) incorporate      (B) immigrate      (C) forge      (D) emerge

( ) 9. I take as little _____ as possible with me when I travel abroad. I like to travel light.

(A) wheat (B) fancy

(C) baggage (D) unemployment

( ) 10. When I visited Tokyo for the first time, I got confused by the complicated rail _____ there.

(A) network (B) framework (C) firework (D) housework

( ) 11. We should learn to look on the bright _____ and have a positive attitude to life.

(A) slice (B) spine (C) sheet (D) side

( ) 12. The people in the war zone are in urgent need of food and medical help. Supplies are almost _____.

(A) eliminated (B) exhausted (C) accelerated (D) preserved

( ) 13. When dealing with his assignments, Bob tends to be too optimistic and _____ the possible difficulties ahead.

(A) overtakes (B) overthrows (C) overturns (D) overlooks

( ) 14. A group of women _____ a campaign against sexual discrimination in the workplace.

(A) flocked (B) rioted (C) launched (D) quoted

( ) 15. A _____ is a large sports ground with seats all around.

(A) studio (B) strip (C) statue (D) stadium

( ) 16. Anna was _____ about the office gossip that her coworkers spread about her.

(A) furious (B) compulsory (C) armed (D) fiscal

( ) 17. When Mila goes camping in the wilderness, she always brings a _____ gas stove with her.

(A) portable (B) measurable (C) variable (D) dim

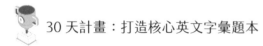 

(     ) 18. The border dispute between the two countries should be understood within the broader _____ of their history.

    (A) context     (B) continent     (C) contest     (D) technician

(     ) 19. I wear this _____ of perfume because I adore its fragrance of wood.

    (A) monk     (B) breed     (C) brand     (D) journalist

(     ) 20. Willy dreamed of winning a lottery, becoming a _____ and enjoying a life of luxury ever after.

    (A) brass     (B) millionaire     (C) breast     (D) contract

## II. Fill in the Blank （從下方選出適合字彙做適當變化，填入答案）

| revenge | honor | circumstance | complain | wave |
|---------|-------|--------------|----------|------|

_____ 1. At the end of the story, the lady took _____ on his husband, who had cheated on her.

_____ 2. After Fiona walked out of the shop, the salesclerk _____ goodbye to her at the door.

_____ 3. We held the dinner party in _____ of a fellow teacher who was going to retire.

_____ 4. Tina is always _____ that her husband is good-for-nothing.

_____ 5. Under no _____ will Annie's father agree with her marrying the old man.

## III. Guided Translation （寫出完整字彙）

1. 體檢完醫生告訴病人這個消息後，他嚇得說不出話來。

The patient was speechless with shock as his doctor b_____ t_____ n_____ t_____ him after the check-up.

2. 女主人講了一些有趣的笑話，試圖讓她的客人感到輕鬆自在。

The hostess tried to make her guests feel a_____ e_____

by telling some funny jokes.

3. Rory 和他的朋友們一路走到火車站，而不是坐計程車。

Rory and his friends walked all the way to the train station r_____

t_____ took a taxi.

4. 除了新聞，我父親幾乎不看電視。

E_____ f_____ news, my father hardly watches

television.

5. 我希望今天下午天氣轉晴，因為我們有一場橄欖球比賽。

I hope the weather c_____ u_____ this afternoon

because we have a football game.

# Round 14

## I. Multiple Choice

(　　) 1. All the workers in this country are guaranteed a(n) _____ wage, and they must not be paid less than that.
    (A) arrogant　　(B) minimum　　(C) most　　(D) eloquent

(　　) 2. The coach called a timeout to let the athlete rest for a few seconds to catch her _____.
    (A) suicide　　(B) index　　(C) habitat　　(D) breath

(　　) 3. The author's latest collection of poems has received favorable reviews from _____ critics.
    (A) literary　　(B) structural　　(C) maximum　　(D) least

(　　) 4. The resident screamed as loudly as she could to give the _____ when the fire broke out.
    (A) fraud　　(B) litter　　(C) motion　　(D) alarm

(　　) 5. The boy is eating a bowl of ice cream _____ with mini marshmallows.
    (A) sprinkled　　(B) disordered　　(C) estimated　　(D) wondered

(　　) 6. The declining birth rate is _____ the country's population, education, and economy.
    (A) inputting　　(B) patting　　(C) attacking　　(D) impacting

(　　) 7. Joseph is good at making bread and cakes because he used to work in a local _____.
    (A) nursery　　(B) bakery　　(C) market　　(D) station

(　) 8. Ellen bought some magnets and key chains as ＿＿＿＿ of her trip to Rome.

    (A) souvenirs　　(B) strategies　　(C) subjects　　(D) solutions

(　) 9. The nation of Israel came into ＿＿＿＿ after World War II.

    (A) reference　　(B) participant　　(C) existence　　(D) bloom

(　) 10. John is very skillful at fixing things around the house and is therefore ＿＿＿＿ "Mr. Handy."

    (A) recognized　　(B) labeled　　(C) nicknamed　　(D) characterized

(　) 11. Most high school students in Taiwan are supposed to go to school in ＿＿＿＿.

    (A) umbrella　　(B) uniform　　(C) unity　　(D) union

(　) 12. Employees who failed to ＿＿＿＿ their obligations were dismissed from their jobs.

    (A) mill　　(B) grill　　(C) fulfill　　(D) drill

(　) 13. This prize will be awarded to any ＿＿＿＿ worker in the scientific field who has made a great discovery.

    (A) spiritual　　(B) evident　　(C) underlying　　(D) outstanding

(　) 14. The police car is going really fast. It must be ＿＿＿＿ somebody.

    (A) sewing　　(B) chasing　　(C) comforting　　(D) stressing

(　) 15. Be careful when you chop vegetables with the knife, for the blade is very ＿＿＿＿.

    (A) sharp　　(B) smooth　　(C) rusty　　(D) explicit

(　) 16. The CEO ＿＿＿＿ the idea as not worthy of consideration.

    (A) searched　　(B) dismissed　　(C) missed　　(D) committed

(　) 17. People have to pay for the ＿＿＿＿ when they send a letter.

    (A) poster　　(B) postcard　　(C) postage　　(D) postponement

(     ) 18. The invention of the cat's eye made a major _____ to road safety.

     (A) decision     (B) distribution     (C) contribution     (D) section

(     ) 19. The landlord got furious when the tenant denied _____ for the damage he had caused to the apartment.

     (A) liability     (B) inquiry     (C) harmony     (D) mortality

(     ) 20. The way my neighbor _____ about others really irritates me.

     (A) communicates          (B) shades

     (C) gossips              (D) dusts

## II. Fill in the Blank （從下方選出適合字彙做適當變化，填入答案）

| side | associate | hunt | economical | watch |
| --- | --- | --- | --- | --- |

_____ 1. Mr. Hill is _____ with his time and money. He never wastes them.

_____ 2. The color red tends to be _____ with good luck in Chinese culture.

_____ 3. The police have been _____ for the missing child in the woods for two days.

_____ 4. The billionaire hired dozens of bodyguards to _____ over him and his family around the clock.

_____ 5. The cough medicine has a(n) _____ effect on my heart, and it is now beating very fast.

## III. Guided Translation （寫出完整字彙）

1. 這餐廳既乾淨又漂亮。最棒的是，它的食物很美味又不貴。

The restaurant is clean and beautiful. B_____ o_____

a_____, its food is delicious and inexpensive.

2. 我突然想到我們可以給爸爸買一把新的電動刮鬍刀作為他的生日禮物。

   It o_____ t_____ me that we could get dad a new electric razor as his birthday present.

3. 我身體不舒服，需要馬上去看醫生。

   I am u_____ t_____ w_____ and need to see a doctor right now.

4. 在比賽中被打敗，Dylan 感到情緒低落。

   Being defeated in the game, Dylan felt d_____ i_____ t_____ d_____ .

5. Gina 花了一個小時才擺脫那個煩人的推銷員。

   It took Gina an hour to g_____ r_____ o_____ the annoying salesman.

# Round 15

## I. Multiple Choice

(       ) 1. The candidate _____ the interviewer with his outstanding self-introduction.
(A) admired       (B) marked       (C) impressed       (D) discouraged

(       ) 2. Go _____ ahead, and you can see the post office on your left.
(A) round       (B) rough       (C) straight       (D) throughout

(       ) 3. The famous _____ has performed numerous successful operations.
(A) surgeon       (B) agent       (C) dealer       (D) producer

(       ) 4. The ballerina danced so _____ that we all fixed our eyes on her.
(A) presumably     (B) gracefully       (C) profoundly       (D) supposedly

(       ) 5. The jobless man turned to _____ and got wasted every day after his wife and children left him.
(A) lemonade       (B) alcohol       (C) vinegar       (D) steam

(       ) 6. Ms. Brown, with her infinite patience, is ideally _____ to teaching small children.
(A) examined       (B) inherited       (C) suited       (D) confused

(       ) 7. The interests and rights of the _____ groups should be respected and protected.
(A) minority       (B) peer       (C) conscience       (D) action

(       ) 8. As Howard was going _____, he looked much older than his real age.
(A) compact       (B) bald       (C) hateful       (D) bold

( ) 9. The courageous lifeguard _____ no fear while saving a drowning boy in the lake.

(A) pleaded     (B) displayed     (C) delayed     (D) threaded

( ) 10. The little girl woke up from a terrifying _____ and couldn't stop crying.

(A) advocate     (B) vision     (C) intuition     (D) nightmare

( ) 11. The driver hit the _____, but to his horror the car did not slow down.

(A) brakes     (B) plates     (C) trunks     (D) breaks

( ) 12. Moving from Finland to Brazil, it took Tyler a year to adapt himself to the new _____.

(A) appointments           (B) stances

(C) morals                 (D) surroundings

( ) 13. Social _____ means all individuals within a certain society enjoy equal liberties, rights, and access to public goods.

(A) extent     (B) ecosystem     (C) equity     (D) expert

( ) 14. Don't forget to pay back the money you _____ Peggy.

(A) browse     (B) lend     (C) loan     (D) owe

( ) 15. I will always _____ the memories of the years I spent with my besties at school.

(A) publish     (B) cherish     (C) switch     (D) recite

( ) 16. Why did the police _____ Gina of committing the murder? I'm sure she is innocent.

(A) release     (B) mention     (C) suspect     (D) approve

( ) 17. _____ with a flashlight, the guard carried out a routine patrol at night.

(A) Furnished     (B) Flushed     (C) Hushed     (D) Polished

(     ) 18. I think the message _____ in the movie is that everyone has to face their death sooner or later.

    (A) translated     (B) transferred     (C) urged     (D) conveyed

(     ) 19. The salvage team used sonar to _____ the shipwreck.

    (A) locate     (B) heal     (C) dodge     (D) abolish

(     ) 20. The Earth is one of the _____ that rotate around the Sun.

    (A) bins     (B) grams     (C) databases     (D) planets

## II. Fill in the Blank （從下方選出適合字彙做適當變化，填入答案）

| block | position | identify | attention | possession |
|---|---|---|---|---|

_____ 1. Noticing Marcus staring into space, the teacher walked toward him and asked him to pay _____.

_____ 2. Do you _____ with the main character's struggle?

_____ 3. I am not the person in charge, so I am in no _____ to give orders.

_____ 4. We should not take the road because it was _____ up by a landslide.

_____ 5. The famous painting by Vincent van Gogh is now in a private collector's _____.

## III. Guided Translation （寫出完整字彙）

1. 這雙靴子下週會特價，到時候你可以以更低的價格入手。

The boots will be o_____ s_____ next week, and you can get them at a lower price then.

2. 多虧了你的幫忙，我們才能按時完成這項艱難的任務。

T_____ t_____ your help, we can complete the difficult task on time.

3. 你能馬上到我辦公室嗎？我有急事要告訴你。

Can you come to my office r_____ a_____ ? I have something urgent to tell you.

4. 實際上是 Leonard 的妻子在經營這家商店。他負責其他業務。

It is Leonard's wife who is i_____ e_____ running the store. He is in charge of other business.

5. 雖然 Ollie 的收入不固定，但她平均每年賺取五萬美元。

Although Ollie's income is variable, he earns US$50,000 a year o_____ a_____ .

# Round 16

## I. Multiple Choice

(　　) 1. Severe _____ are placed on the sale of alcohol in the country.
　　　　(A) descriptions　(B) participants　(C) restrictions　(D) instructions

(　　) 2. The collector displays her valuable pieces of china in a glass-fronted
　　　　_____.
　　　　(A) cabin　　　(B) cabinet　　(C) cable　　　(D) cafeteria

(　　) 3. Out of _____, out of mind. If you don't see something, you will
　　　　easily forget all about it.
　　　　(A) height　　　(B) knight　　(C) might　　　(D) sight

(　　) 4. Jasmine _____ her head while she was solving the difficult math
　　　　problem.
　　　　(A) scratched　(B) poked　　(C) pumped　　(D) omitted

(　　) 5. In persuasive writing, you have to provide enough _____ arguments
　　　　to support your points of view.
　　　　(A) frightened　(B) logical　　(C) insane　　(D) concerned

(　　) 6. The public is very _____ to the dangers of building a nuclear power
　　　　plant in the city.
　　　　(A) alert　　　(B) aware　　(C) timid　　　(D) statistical

(　　) 7. A cup of black coffee in the morning enables Zoe to _____ awake
　　　　all day.
　　　　(A) consider　　(B) apply　　(C) stay　　　(D) quit

(　　) 8. These students' test scores _____ that they had studied very hard.
　　　　(A) supplied　　(B) implied　　(C) reassured　(D) replied

(    ) 9. You should not expect any _____. Success will come only through hard work.

(A) missiles      (B) miracles      (C) mysteries      (D) mentors

(    ) 10. The boy fell down and hurt his left knee, so his mother put a _____ on it.

(A) bandage      (B) cover      (C) brick      (D) cone

(    ) 11. In order to kill pests, the farmer _____ the crops with pesticide every two months.

(A) dyes      (B) dries      (C) smashes      (D) sprays

(    ) 12. The question was hotly _____ in the board meeting.

(A) deployed      (B) overseen      (C) proclaimed      (D) disputed

(    ) 13. The prophet's theory about the end of the world is complete _____ to me. I don't believe a word of it.

(A) logic      (B) evidence      (C) scenario      (D) nonsense

(    ) 14. The _____ firefighter risked his life to rescue those trapped in the collapsed building.

(A) shameful      (B) suspicious      (C) brave      (D) nonprofit

(    ) 15. The _____ erupted yesterday. Thus, the nearby villages were covered with ash.

(A) waterfall      (B) circumstance      (C) pledge      (D) volcano

(    ) 16. Ben's parents were both musicians. As a result, he was _____ to music at an early age.

(A) recorded      (B) touched      (C) concealed      (D) exposed

(    ) 17. I just made some general comments. Don't take them _____, otherwise you will feel upset.

(A) privately      (B) personally      (C) abruptly      (D) roughly

(    ) 18. The birds that were _____ outside woke me up at daybreak.

(A) banging      (B) booming      (C) whistling      (D) swaying

(    ) 19. In the pop concert, the audience _____ at the unexpected guest in amazement.

      (A) stared      (B) managed      (C) nominated      (D) dissolved

(    ) 20. The species of butterflies are not _____ to this area. They come from South America.

      (A) indigenous      (B) legendary      (C) secondary      (D) viable

## II. Fill in the Blank （從下方選出適合字彙做適當變化，填入答案）

| peak | impression | element | ride | serve |
|------|------------|---------|------|-------|

_____ 1. The living room also _____ as our dining place.

_____ 2. It's quite late now. Could you give me a(n) _____ to the train station?

_____ 3. Booking a plane ticket at the _____ of the holiday season is not easy.

_____ 4. There is a(n) _____ of truth in Jimmy's story. A small part of what he said is true.

_____ 5. Mindy was under the _____ that Grace worked for a government organization.

## III. Guided Translation （寫出完整字彙）

1. 天氣原本晴朗，但突然間，烏雲密佈開始且下起雨來。

The weather was sunny, but a_____ a_____ o_____, dark clouds gathered and it started to rain.

2. 如果你在街上偶然遇到你的偶像，你會對他或她說什麼？

P_____ t_____ you run into your idol on the street, what would you say to him or her?

3. 部門會議什麼時候舉行？

What time will the departmental meeting t_____ p_____?

4. 你在發高燒。我建議你盡快去看醫生。

You are running a high fever. I suggest you see a doctor a_____ s_____ a_____ p_____.

5. 相較於藍色後背包，綠色的容量較大。

I_____ c_____ w_____ the blue backpack, the green one is more capacious.

# Round 17

## I. Multiple Choice

(　　) 1. People who do ＿＿＿＿ jobs usually have to work by physical strength.
　　(A) exterior　　(B) dangerous　　(C) manual　　(D) elaborate

(　　) 2. These works of art are ＿＿＿＿ of the local artists' talents and creativity.
　　(A) narrative　　(B) envious　　(C) sensible　　(D) representative

(　　) 3. The insurance agent didn't return my calls. I don't think she is ＿＿＿＿ in helping me.
　　(A) sincere　　(B) fragile　　(C) dishonest　　(D) dreadful

(　　) 4. The online shop ＿＿＿＿ to offer high-quality products at bargain prices.
　　(A) recommends　　(B) ignores　　(C) flatters　　(D) guarantees

(　　) 5. Joe's parents give him such a small ＿＿＿＿ so that he has to earn extra money by taking a part-time job.
　　(A) celebration　　(B) album　　(C) allowance　　(D) fossil

(　　) 6. After dinner, Sophia likes to walk along the ＿＿＿＿ of the lake with her husband.
　　(A) shore　　(B) archive　　(C) chore　　(D) robber

(　　) 7. Taiwan is very hot and ＿＿＿＿ in summer, especially in July and August.
　　(A) humid　　(B) brass　　(C) guilty　　(D) mild

(　) 8. The boy played practical jokes on his classmates with his eyes full of _____ .

(A) morality　(B) mischief　(C) compassion　(D) relaxation

(　) 9. Let's drink a _____ to the newly married couple!

(A) report　(B) stroke　(C) feast　(D) toast

(　) 10. Sam cannot _____ one color from another. He is color-blind.

(A) dislike　(B) distinguish　(C) distribute　(D) disrupt

(　) 11. It is _____ for young children to be curious and keep asking questions about things around them.

(A) habitual　(B) unusual　(C) conventional　(D) normal

(　) 12. The health minister _____ live to the nation at 2 p.m. every day during the pandemic.

(A) explores　(B) programs　(C) broadcasts　(D) encourages

(　) 13. With the invention of the washing machine, people can do the _____ with ease.

(A) laundry　(B) lifeguard　(C) vacuum　(D) pension

(　) 14. Never pursue profit at the _____ of safety.

(A) expansion　(B) expedition　(C) experience　(D) expense

(　) 15. Plants produce _____ during the day and help to clean the air humans breathe.

(A) wilderness　(B) custody　(C) oxygen　(D) moisture

(　) 16. I mistook Molly for her sister at the party because they bore a _____ similarity.

(A) commercial　(B) potential　(C) sturdy　(D) striking

(　) 17. On my way to school, I saw a _____ of workers repairing the road.

(A) gun　(B) gum　(C) gang　(D) grain

(     ) 18. To have healthy babies, women are advised to stop drinking and smoking during _____.

(A) frequency     (B) pregnancy     (C) vacancy     (D) accuracy

(     ) 19. Emily pays for her insurance _____ with a credit card on a monthly basis.

(A) defendant     (B) genre     (C) ideology     (D) premium

(     ) 20. For Fred, it is a challenging task to _____ his stubborn father to change his mind.

(A) convince     (B) converse     (C) contrast     (D) convey

## II. Fill in the Blank （從下方選出適合字彙做適當變化，填入答案）

| fear | pick | mess | catch | pride |
|------|------|------|-------|-------|

_____ 1. Why do you _____ on me all the time? I've had enough!

_____ 2. Elliot must have _____ a cold too, for he has the same symptoms as yours.

_____ 3. A: Can I borrow your car for the weekend?

B: Absolutely not! You always make a _____ in my car.

_____ 4. The old couple took _____ in their son's achievements.

_____ 5. Rowan didn't dare to tell his father the news for _____ that he might fly into a rage.

## III. Guided Translation （寫出完整字彙）

1. 我一到紐西蘭就會打電話給你。

I'll g_____ you a c_____ as soon as I arrive in New Zealand.

2. 如果發生緊急事件請按鈴。

Please ring the bell i_____ c_____ o_____ emergency.

3. 在戰爭的陰影下，該國的經濟情勢越來越糟。

The economic situation in the country has g_____ f_____ b_____ t_____ w_____ under the shadow of the war.

4. Lucas 總以看棒球比賽為樂。

Lucas always t_____ d_____ i_____ watching baseball games.

5. 今早的討論過程中，其中一名員工提出一個關於新品發布會的絕佳主意。

During the discussion this morning, one of the employees c_____ u_____ w_____ a brilliant idea about the new product launch.

# Round 18

## I. Multiple Choice

(      ) 1. The hotel business _____ after the outbreak of the contagious disease.

    (A) collapsed     (B) burst     (C) erected     (D) parachuted

(      ) 2. Whenever Theo reads a book, he writes his comments in the _____.

    (A) whites     (B) insights     (C) bruises     (D) margins

(      ) 3. The basic _____ of an English composition is different from that of a Chinese composition.

    (A) exhibition     (B) triumph     (C) jewelry     (D) structure

(      ) 4. The entire nation was _____ over the death of the soldiers in the war.

    (A) grieving     (B) believing     (C) relieving     (D) deceiving

(      ) 5. The plot of the play bears some _____ to that of *Hamlet*. They are both about a prince taking revenge on his father's killer.

    (A) placements     (B) similarities     (C) standards     (D) qualities

(      ) 6. The golfer won the tournament at the age of 23 when he was still an _____ rather than a professional.

    (A) agent     (B) amateur     (C) activist     (D) administrator

(      ) 7. Lauren was once a legal _____ before she went into the entertainment industry. She used to represent clients in a court of law.

    (A) practitioner     (B) sensor     (C) pioneer     (D) slave

(    ) 8. This organization is meant to help those _____ children who suffer from domestic violence.

(A) accidental    (B) terrific    (C) miserable    (D) sufficient

(    ) 9. The study has proven the _____ that students who have breakfast will perform better than those who don't.

(A) hypothesis    (B) forum    (C) portfolio    (D) sponsorship

(    ) 10. There is a man with _____ hair on the doorstep. Do you know who he is?

(A) skinny    (B) silent    (C) shady    (D) silver

(    ) 11. The heartbroken woman _____ her husband because he was on drugs and didn't have a regular job.

(A) digested    (B) proposed    (C) engaged    (D) divorced

(    ) 12. I always keep a pen and paper on hand so that I can take _____ whenever I need to.

(A) notes    (B) notices    (C) writings    (D) replies

(    ) 13. The teacher was sued because he gave his student a _____ beating.

(A) soft    (B) brutal    (C) chronic    (D) tender

(    ) 14. We haven't heard from Miranda since we _____ from high school.

(A) hesitated    (B) gazed    (C) remained    (D) graduated

(    ) 15. There are several beautifully wrapped _____ lying around the Christmas tree.

(A) sausages    (B) hostages    (C) packages    (D) patches

(    ) 16. Tobby sang the solo part, and the rest of the band members joined in the _____ harmoniously.

(A) chorus    (B) orchestra    (C) symptom    (D) chamber

(    ) 17. The weather was so hot that the marathon runner _____ a lot.

(A) married    (B) sucked    (C) sweated    (D) floated

(     ) 18. There is a wide _____ between the rich and the poor in the country.
    (A) hop     (B) gap     (C) tap     (D) sip

(     ) 19. Before the refrigerator was invented, people used to _____ food by drying it in the sun or soaking it in salt.
    (A) reserve     (B) obtain     (C) preserve     (D) object

(     ) 20. It is the custom for children to wear _____ to collect candies on Halloween.
    (A) ruins     (B) translations     (C) hoses     (D) costumes

## II. Fill in the Blank （從下方選出適合字彙做適當變化，填入答案）

| emphasis | balance | command | inferior | compare |
|---|---|---|---|---|

_____ 1. My teacher puts great _____ on the ability to speak English. Therefore, we usually practice speaking English in class.

_____ 2. We must strike a(n) _____ between reckless spending and penny pinching.

_____ 3. Generally speaking, instant coffee is _____ to fresh coffee in taste. That's why it is much cheaper.

_____ 4. According to Greek mythology, Helen's beauty was beyond _____. Even goddesses envied her beauty.

_____ 5. These foot soldiers were _____ not to give in when fighting against the enemy in the war.

## III. Guided Translation （寫出完整字彙）

1. 機場一度因為淹水而關閉，但現在開始營運了。

The airport was once closed because of the flood, but it c_____ i_____ u_____ now.

2. 那位歷史學者昨晚離世了。他的葬禮將在下週舉行。

The history scholar p_____ a_____ last night. His funeral will be held next week.

3. 依我所見，從事極限運動的人冒著負傷與喪命的風險。

In my opinion, people who do extreme sports t_____ t_____ r_____ o_____ getting injured or being killed.

4. A：不知道你是否願意和我去舞會嗎？

B：可以下次嗎？我今晚剛好有預約我牙醫的門診。

A: I'm wondering if you'd like to go to the dance with me?

B: May I t_____ a r_____ c_____? I happen to have an appointment with my dentist tonight.

5. 新的交通法規將於七月一號生效。

The new traffic regulations will c_____ i_____ e_____ on July 1.

# Round 19

## I. Multiple Choice

(     ) 1. Freya always tells her _____ friend about everything that troubles her.

     (A) optional      (B) intimate      (C) historic      (D) trivial

(     ) 2. The aim of this law is to _____ gender inequality in the workplace.

     (A) multiply      (B) empty      (C) survey      (D) eliminate

(     ) 3. The medical experiment involved _____ with some top universities like Harvard University and Oxford University.

     (A) subsidy      (B) collaboration      (C) franchise      (D) deficit

(     ) 4. Airline passengers must keep their _____ either under their seats or in the overhead bins.

     (A) luggage      (B) account      (C) fragment      (D) passage

(     ) 5. _____, the woman was frozen with fear when someone broke into her house.

     (A) Disappointed      (B) Delighted      (C) Twisted      (D) Shocked

(     ) 6. Many _____ reached the front line of the war to offer their help selflessly.

     (A) statues      (B) robots      (C) volunteers      (D) landlords

(     ) 7. Ruby had her hair cut and dyed at the newly opened hair _____ on King Street.

     (A) cocaine      (B) criterion      (C) bin      (D) salon

(     ) 8. It is unkind of you to laugh at other people's _____.

     (A) absence      (B) humor      (C) misfortune      (D) success

(　　) 9. This silk shirt is 60% off, and it was a real _____ .

    (A) fluid     (B) estate     (C) entertainment (D) bargain

(　　) 10. I saw Roger several minutes ago. He must be _____ in the building now.

    (A) somewhere   (B) somewhat   (C) somehow   (D) sometimes

(　　) 11. The Romans once _____ Europe. They had control over a large part of the continent.

    (A) dominated   (B) ruined     (C) rebuilt     (D) established

(　　) 12. The cost of living is much higher these days, so it's hard to keep within _____ .

    (A) budget     (B) fund     (C) agriculture   (D) venture

(　　) 13. Sophie _____ the fairy tale in five sentences.

    (A) scouted     (B) succeeded   (C) summarized   (D) supported

(　　) 14. The gardener is trimming the bushes with a huge _____ of scissors.

    (A) piece     (B) pair     (C) couple     (D) clap

(　　) 15. The bad news _____ around the whole town very quickly.

    (A) elected     (B) circulated   (C) extended     (D) arrived

(　　) 16. The firefighters tried hard to stop the fire from _____ .

    (A) enabling     (B) sheltering   (C) devoting     (D) spreading

(　　) 17. In recent years, the government has reduced _____ on the import of Japanese cars to boost the local car industry.

    (A) icons     (B) quotas     (C) loops     (D) venues

(　　) 18. With the final exams coming, the students are under great _____ to finish studying for all of them.

    (A) force     (B) power     (C) pressure     (D) relief

(　　) 19. Cigarette smoke always makes me _____ , so I try to stay away from smokers.

    (A) imitate     (B) draft     (C) cough     (D) laugh

(　　) 20. Ian accused Amber of posting a(n) _____ rumor about him on the Internet.

     (A) false       (B) identical     (C) plastic     (D) lawful

## II. Fill in the Blank （從下方選出適合字彙做適當變化，填入答案）

| infect | reach | commit | concentrate | steal |
|--------|-------|--------|-------------|-------|

_____ 1. The woman _____ a serious crime and spent the rest of her life behind bars.

_____ 2. The white-collar worker was accused of _____ money from her coworker this morning.

_____ 3. The majority of the local residents were _____ with some kind of bacteria, and one of them was even dying.

_____ 4. If you want to pass the English proficiency test, you'll have to _____ on practicing listening skills.

_____ 5. Both sides finally _____ a settlement. The driver needed to pay the victim of the car accident NT$50,000.

## III. Guided Translation （寫出完整字彙）

1. 為了償還債務，Frank 必須割捨他的車子。

To p_____ o_____ his debts, Frank had to part with his car.

2. White 先生堅定的意志驅使他每天早上去公園慢跑，風雨無阻。

Mr. White's strong will drives him to go jogging in the park every morning, r_____ o_____ s_____.

3. 這名年輕人遭身體虐待好幾年。

The young man has been p_____ a_____ for several years.

4. 這個計畫不切實際。它永遠不可能付諸實行。

This plan is only a pie in the sky. It can never be p_____

i_____ p_____.

5. 這部電影取材於十九世紀一名金礦工人的真實故事。

The film is b_____ o_____ a true story of a gold miner in the 19th century.

# Round 20

## I. Multiple Choice

(　　) 1. The boss asked the _____ to keep the files on the clients in alphabetical order.
   (A) container　　(B) infant　　(C) prophet　　(D) assistant

(　　) 2. Please don't _____ the contents of the contract to others. We have to keep them secret.
   (A) scramble　　(B) expect　　(C) torture　　(D) reveal

(　　) 3. Ted's jacket is _____ to mine. They are both dark blue in color.
   (A) similar　　(B) familiar　　(C) related　　(D) apparent

(　　) 4. Quick! Call a(n) _____! I think the man is having a heart attack.
   (A) ambulance　　　　　　(B) announcement
   (C) earphone　　　　　　(D) trigger

(　　) 5. Susan was the only _____ of the train crash. All other passengers on board were killed.
   (A) victim　　(B) survivor　　(C) controversy　　(D) excitement

(　　) 6. Ms. Sullivan is a religious Christian who lives in _____ to Christian teachings.
   (A) courtesy　　(B) obedience　　(C) slavery　　(D) temper

(　　) 7. For Sam, the fear of talking to strangers is the biggest _____ to making new friends.
   (A) barrier　　(B) emotion　　(C) youngster　　(D) captain

(　　) 8. Ray had an upset _____ shortly after eating unclean food in the night market.
   (A) nose　　(B) lung　　(C) liver　　(D) stomach

( ) 9. Since I have no _____ talent, I am poor at acting.

    (A) democratic    (B) realistic    (C) dramatic    (D) critical

( ) 10. My grandfather is a liberal person and is always open-minded about any _____ ideas.

    (A) nasty    (B) voluntary    (C) novel    (D) recent

( ) 11. Without a ladder, it is impossible for Jeffrey to change the _____ on the ceiling.

    (A) floor    (B) bulb    (C) carpet    (D) furniture

( ) 12. The boat was about to _____ , so the passengers put on their life vests quickly.

    (A) kick    (B) sink    (C) trick    (D) wink

( ) 13. The young girl often _____ herself as a fashion model walking on a runway.

    (A) leads    (B) links    (C) fancies    (D) confuses

( ) 14. All the zebras fled in _____ as soon as they saw the lions approaching.

    (A) pleasure    (B) patience    (C) panic    (D) grief

( ) 15. But for your _____ , I would have lost a large sum of money in the stock market.

    (A) warning    (B) appreciation    (C) curse    (D) stereotype

( ) 16. Some doctors _____ upon a diet which contains only fruit and vegetables.

    (A) oppose    (B) rebel    (C) pause    (D) frown

( ) 17. Ben is determined to win the race and nothing can _____ him from achieving his goal.

    (A) overcome    (B) disapprove    (C) prevent    (D) defend

(      ) 18. The sales figures in the third quarter of the year roughly _____ to what they had predicted.

(A) replied      (B) corresponded (C) devoted      (D) condemned

(      ) 19. The politician's behavior is not _____ with his words.

(A) consistent      (B) neutral      (C) probable      (D) truthful

(      ) 20. _____ of a man following her all the way, Cindy hastily ran into the nearest convenience store.

(A) Compassionate      (B) Embarrassed

(C) Municipal      (D) Conscious

## II. Fill in the Blank （從下方選出適合字彙做適當變化，填入答案）

| roll | instant | wear | record | inform |
|------|---------|------|--------|--------|

_____ 1. Keep me _____ of the changes in the stock prices. Don't let me miss the opportunity to make a fortune.

_____ 2. The scientists keep a(n) _____ of the Earth's movements every day.

_____ 3. The intensive training has _____ the baseball players out.

_____ 4. The teacher called the _____ to see who was absent this morning.

_____ 5. The _____ that the wanted man saw the policeman, he ran away.

## III. Guided Translation （寫出完整字彙）

1. Sandy 在大學畢業後與 Mia 失去聯繫。

Sandy l_____ t_____ w_____ Mia after they graduated from college.

2. 由於 Ivy 再也無法忍受她老闆的無禮行為，她將於明天辭職。

As Ivy cannot p_____ u_____ w_____ her

boss's rude behavior anymore, she will quit her job tomorrow.

3. 那位老先生被汽車撞倒，並馬上被送往醫院。

The old man was knocked down by a car and was sent to the hospital

i_____ n_____ t_____ .

4. 「禁止游泳」的警告標誌被設置於湖邊

A warning sign saying "No Swimming" is s_____ u_____

by the lake.

5. 你必須非常小心，否則你最後可能會在活動中受傷。

You must be very careful, or you may e_____ u_____

getting hurt in the activity.

# Round 21

## I. Multiple Choice

(　　) 1. The audience was _____ at the tricks performed by the circus last night.
(A) minimized　(B) squeezed　(C) realized　(D) amazed

(　　) 2. My supervisor and _____ sighed with relief when the work was finished in time.
(A) colleagues　(B) conductors　(C) composers　(D) collectors

(　　) 3. The workers on the night _____ work from midnight to the early morning.
(A) manner　(B) legacy　(C) condition　(D) shift

(　　) 4. You cannot park your car in this area. It's _____ for people with disabilities.
(A) reserved　(B) emerged　(C) split　(D) melted

(　　) 5. The wealthy celebrity owns a lot of _____ goods such as jewelry and designer bags.
(A) deputy　(B) luxury　(C) currency　(D) community

(　　) 6. After _____ the situation, we had a clear idea about what we should do next.
(A) padding　(B) concluding　(C) analyzing　(D) remedying

(　　) 7. The bride's huge diamond ring _____ brightly in the sun.
(A) shot　(B) shocked　(C) shut　(D) shone

(　　) 8. Liam always gets his _____ from the poems written by Robert Frost.
(A) introduction　(B) installation　(C) inspiration　(D) instruction

(   ) 9. When Steve came home, he found his house had been broken into and all the gold watches were _____.

(A) missing     (B) ongoing     (C) promising     (D) cunning

(   ) 10. After the cleaner cleaned the mop, he _____ the dirty water into a ditch.

(A) assigned     (B) murdered     (C) poured     (D) buried

(   ) 11. Karen is on an economy _____ now and is doing her best to cut down on her expenses.

(A) hostility     (B) taste     (C) drive     (D) case

(   ) 12. Public concern is still about the negative effect a _____ power plant may bring about on the environment.

(A) native     (B) nuclear     (C) nutritious     (D) narrow

(   ) 13. The townspeople held a _____ in honor of the baseball team that had just won the championship.

(A) riot     (B) hike     (C) parade     (D) protest

(   ) 14. On Valentine's Day, Henry sent his girlfriend a _____ of red roses to express his love for her.

(A) bucket     (B) barrel     (C) bottle     (D) bunch

(   ) 15. The books in the library are _____ according to the subjects.

(A) spilled     (B) classified     (C) formed     (D) generated

(   ) 16. The dress designer often reads magazines about the _____ fashion to keep herself up to date.

(A) last     (B) latest     (C) later     (D) latter

(   ) 17. The entrepreneur does everything in his _____. He never follows what others do.

(A) victory     (B) kingdom     (C) range     (D) fashion

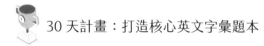

(     ) 18. I have forgotten what we talked about in the _____ conversation. Can you help me refresh my memory?

　　(A) previous　　(B) premier　　(C) passionate　　(D) pathetic

(     ) 19. Whenever the director feels depressed, he goes to the countryside and goes on a _____ in the woods.

　　(A) defeat　　(B) retreat　　(C) repeat　　(D) threat

(     ) 20. A trademark creates an image for a product and can be a good marketing _____.

　　(A) device　　(B) supply　　(C) topic　　(D) lounge

## II. Fill in the Blank （從下方選出適合字彙做適當變化，填入答案）

| result | consequence | polish | interfere | room |
|--------|-------------|--------|-----------|------|

_____ 1. Car exhaust fumes _____ in air pollution.

_____ 2. Harper missed the school bus this morning and, in _____, she was late for school.

_____ 3. To make _____ for her new clothes, Melissa donated some of her old ones to a local charity.

_____ 4. It is not wise of Martha to _____ in her neighbor's business.

_____ 5. I have to _____ up my French before I go on a trip to Paris.

## III. Guided Translation （寫出完整字彙）

1. 孩子們經常在農曆新年假期放鞭炮。

   Children often s_____ o_____ firecrackers during the Chinese New Year holidays.

2. Ben 辭職後，他又再次回學校讀書。

   After Ben quit his job, he went back to school to study o_____ a_____.

3. 消防員來了五分鐘後，火被撲滅了。

Five minutes after the firefighters came, the fire was p_____

o_____.

4. 因為暴風雨，小船翻覆了。

B_____ o_____ the storm, the small boat was tipped

over.

5. 這個學校的大多數人都認為 Owen 先生是他們遇過最好的老師。

Most people in the school t_____ o_____ Mr. Owen as

the best teacher they have ever met.

# Round 22

## I. Multiple Choice

(     ) 1. Some people believe installing surveillance cameras is a violation of
_____ .

     (A) disability      (B) cruelty      (C) efficiency      (D) privacy

(     ) 2. Ivy is not used to having physical _____ with strangers. Even a
handshake makes her uneasy.

     (A) output      (B) contact      (C) circuit      (D) dignity

(     ) 3. The news report said that two policemen and a criminal were killed in
the shooting _____ last night.

     (A) incident      (B) assembly      (C) impression      (D) convention

(     ) 4. Humankind has been using fire since _____ times.

     (A) ancient      (B) spare      (C) precious      (D) romantic

(     ) 5. The police officer _____ the thief by the arm and took him to the
police station.

     (A) adopted      (B) schemed      (C) seized      (D) attended

(     ) 6. Skyler _____ the whole wheat cereal in milk and then had it for
brunch.

     (A) drummed      (B) drowned      (C) drunk      (D) drained

(     ) 7. The nun firmly believes that her _____ in life is to help the poor.

     (A) mission      (B) recession      (C) celebration      (D) admission

(     ) 8. The bear caught fish with its _____ in the river.

     (A) fur      (B) thigh      (C) tissue      (D) paw

(    ) 9. At the end of every month, my pocket money left is _____.

    (A) scary      (B) severe      (C) secure      (D) scarce

(    ) 10. Traffic on the highway was _____ for hours by the car accident.

    (A) halted      (B) conducted      (C) destroyed      (D) improved

(    ) 11. Buying a house usually places a heavy financial _____ on young couples.

    (A) bundle      (B) bullet      (C) burden      (D) bureau

(    ) 12. The drug scandal was _____ to the senator's reputation.

    (A) fearful      (B) fantastic      (C) favorite      (D) fatal

(    ) 13. It is required by the law that all the _____ in a car must fasten their seat belts.

    (A) foreigners      (B) passengers      (C) practitioners      (D) diplomats

(    ) 14. Keep your fingers away from the crab's _____ when you pick it up.

    (A) clauses      (B) claps      (C) claws      (D) clashes

(    ) 15. Working long hours every day, the ambitious actor risked his health in _____ of fame and wealth in Hollywood.

    (A) postage      (B) presentation      (C) perception      (D) pursuit

(    ) 16. The pizza looked so tasty that Mark couldn't _____ the temptation to bite it.

    (A) assist      (B) insist      (C) resist      (D) persist

(    ) 17. When I was a kid, my mother often taught me the virtue of _____ through fables and fairy tales.

    (A) honesty      (B) tension      (C) function      (D) participation

(    ) 18. People should have the _____ to stand up for their beliefs.

    (A) rejection      (B) creativity      (C) courage      (D) gratitude

(     ) 19. It is ironic that human beings have invented _____ to make life easier but end up living a much busier life.

     (A) behavior     (B) machinery     (C) horizon     (D) photography

(     ) 20. Only a few people live on the remote island. The _____ is about 3,000.

     (A) declaration     (B) recreation     (C) imitation     (D) population

## II. Fill in the Blank （從下方選出適合字彙做適當變化，填入答案）

| content | width | headline | willing | lesson |
|---|---|---|---|---|

_____ 1. The volunteers are _____ to offer their help after the powerful earthquake.

_____ 2. Once the Queen's death news came out, it made _____ around the country.

_____ 3. I'm _____ with my present job. I don't want to change jobs at the moment.

_____ 4. The road in front of our school is 5 meters in _____.

_____ 5. Ellie has to learn her _____ today. I hope she won't do anything stupid again.

## III. Guided Translation （寫出完整字彙）

1. 當地政府將拆除這棟老屋，改建一棟新的辦公大樓。

The local government will p_____ d_____ the old house and build a new office building instead.

2. 感謝你的建議。我會銘記在心。

Thank you for your advice. I'll b_____ it i_____ m_____.

3. 人生不太可能稱心如意。總會有不愉快的事情發生。

Life is not likely to be a b_____ o_____
r_____. There is always something unpleasant happening.

4. 儘管在過去的六個月裡付出了很多努力，但計畫仍然失敗了。

The project still failed even though a lot of e_____ had been
p_____ i_____ it over the past six months.

5. 無論執行長再忙，他從未忘記關心妻兒。

No matter how busy the CEO is, he has never l_____
s_____ o_____ his concern for his wife and children.

# Round 23

## I. Multiple Choice

(    ) 1. The couple's marriage ended in divorce owing to their different political and religious _____ .
(A) kettles      (B) beliefs      (C) pajamas      (D) cliffs

(    ) 2. The _____ earthquake last night was the greatest disaster we had ever experienced.
(A) tolerable      (B) massive      (C) deaf      (D) mental

(    ) 3. When Joanna got home, she was _____ to find that her briefcase was left behind on the bus.
(A) messy      (B) usual      (C) horrible      (D) annoyed

(    ) 4. There are four _____ in the word "transportation," and we stress the third one.
(A) metaphors            (B) pronunciations
(C) syllables             (D) scores

(    ) 5. The strawberries are _____ enough for us to pick now.
(A) rare      (B) precise      (C) ripe      (D) vital

(    ) 6. It is difficult for the developing country to strike a balance between _____ development and environmental protection.
(A) comparable    (B) ultimate      (C) alternate      (D) industrial

(    ) 7. Mr. Roy is applying for a green card to become a _____ resident in the United States.
(A) concrete      (B) permanent      (C) stormy      (D) poisonous

( ) 8. Many local residents gathered in the town _____ to talk face-to-face with the mayor.

    (A) hall         (B) toll         (C) doll         (D) fall

( ) 9. Ms. Green was _____ of her purse in the park this morning. Her loss included one hundred dollars and two credit cards.

    (A) identified     (B) qualified     (C) robbed     (D) denied

( ) 10. The witness to the gas explosion was struck _____ with horror. He was incapable of speaking for several minutes.

    (A) dumb       (B) diverse     (C) religious     (D) muddy

( ) 11. Do you think it is good for students to be absolutely _____ without making any objections in any case?

    (A) innocent     (B) systematic     (C) obedient     (D) mathematical

( ) 12. On entering the shower room, William undid the _____ of his shirt swiftly.

    (A) buttons     (B) collars     (C) sleeves     (D) pockets

( ) 13. The leather jacket Alvin bought cost NT$23,000. It is nearly half of my monthly _____.

    (A) abortion     (B) salary     (C) hardware     (D) identity

( ) 14. The results showed that fifty votes were in _____ of the bill, and three were against it.

    (A) expression     (B) favor     (C) honor     (D) landscape

( ) 15. Monica never expresses herself and only _____ takes whatever is offered to her.

    (A) passively     (B) positively     (C) actively     (D) earnestly

( ) 16. We think Richard is intelligent, for he has a(n) _____ plan for getting us out of our difficulties.

    (A) obscure     (B) stupid     (C) dull     (D) clever

(     ) 17. The aim of a commercial is to catch _____ attention and attract them to the product.

    (A) consultants'    (B) economists'    (C) lecturers'    (D) consumers'

(     ) 18. Sara is on a diet, but the cake looks so _____ that she'd like to have a piece.

    (A) tempting    (B) rude    (C) spicy    (D) drowsy

(     ) 19. The students were asked to rehearse the play repeatedly until their _____ was perfect.

    (A) insurance    (B) assurance    (C) performance    (D) tolerance

(     ) 20. Most of the members of congress voted against an increase in the _____ budget because they didn't think there would be any threat of war in the near future.

    (A) constitutional    (B) agricultural    (C) federal    (D) military

## II. Fill in the Blank （從下方選出適合字彙做適當變化，填入答案）

| involve | dress | name | excel | breath |
|---------|-------|------|-------|--------|

_____ 1. I found that reasoning with that stubborn man is just wasting my _____.

_____ 2. The criminal was sent to prison because he was _____ in the robbery.

_____ 3. Leo _____ in running. He is the fastest runner in his school.

_____ 4. It is not nice of you to call him _____ like that. After all, he is your brother.

_____ 5. The lady _____ up for the royal banquet, only to discover that she had forgotten her invitation.

## III. Guided Translation（寫出完整字彙）

1. 我討厭和你爭論這些。我希望我們能一勞永逸地解決爭端。

   I hate having these arguments with you. I hope we can settle the dispute

   o＿＿＿＿＿ a＿＿＿＿＿ f＿＿＿＿＿ a＿＿＿＿＿.

2. 這名街頭藝人似乎有魔力，所有的路人都被她吸引了。

   The street performer s＿＿＿＿＿ t＿＿＿＿＿ possess such a

   magical power that all the passers-by are attracted to her.

3. 那些專家花了大量的時間進行此計畫。

   Those experts have taken a g＿＿＿＿＿ d＿＿＿＿＿

   o＿＿＿＿＿ time to work on the project.

4. A：你不覺得這部電影很刺激嗎？

   B：正好相反，大部分時間我都昏昏欲睡。

   A: Didn't you find the film exciting?

   B: O＿＿＿＿＿ t＿＿＿＿＿ c＿＿＿＿＿, I felt sleepy most

   of the time.

5. 那隻虎斑貓的體重增加太多了，幾乎無法通過貓門。

   The tabby cat has p＿＿＿＿＿ o＿＿＿＿＿ so much

   w＿＿＿＿＿ that it can't nearly get through the cat door.

# Round 24

## I. Multiple Choice

(　　) 1. The elderly patient didn't swallow his food _____ and choked as a result.

    (A) properly    (B) prominently   (C) coarsely    (D) gratefully

(　　) 2. The ambitious man abandoned his family to _____ fame and fortune.

    (A) reject    (B) desert    (C) pursue    (D) punch

(　　) 3. From the hotel room windows, you can get a(n) _____ view of the distant mountains and the beautiful lake down below.

    (A) thoughtful    (B) enthusiastic  (C) magnificent  (D) cautious

(　　) 4. With the approach of the college entrance exam, Leo was filled with _____.

    (A) acquisition    (B) refusal    (C) marble    (D) anxiety

(　　) 5. Everyone in the room _____ in terror when they felt the ground shaking.

    (A) screamed    (B) scratched    (C) scrapped    (D) scrubbed

(　　) 6. Because of high _____, everything costs twice as much as last month.

    (A) diligence    (B) selfishness  (C) inflation    (D) attraction

(　　) 7. We can only afford to stay in a _____ hotel. The luxurious ones are beyond our means.

    (A) modern    (B) moderate    (C) middle    (D) memorial

(　　) 8. Did you hear the noises made by the crickets outside our _____ ?

    (A) tent     (B) sake     (C) carnival     (D) beast

(　　) 9. The store sells a wide _____ of hats. You can always find the exact hat you want.

    (A) construction     (B) decoration     (C) examination     (D) selection

(　　) 10. Emily had to pay customs _____ for her perfume and liquor at the airport.

    (A) notes     (B) penalties     (C) marches     (D) duties

(　　) 11. It is important for a reporter to make _____ reports of facts instead of passing judgments on others.

    (A) protective     (B) active     (C) objective     (D) explosive

(　　) 12. The bee _____ from flower to flower in the garden.

    (A) escaped     (B) analyzed     (C) swept     (D) buzzed

(　　) 13. Nobody wants to be friends with the _____ girl because she only cares about herself.

    (A) influential     (B) fabulous     (C) prosperous     (D) selfish

(　　) 14. Max sprained his _____ while playing basketball, and the doctor asked him to rest for a week.

    (A) ankle     (B) jungle     (C) timetable     (D) bubble

(　　) 15. If you travel to a foreign country, you should bring your _____ with you.

    (A) prospect     (B) passport     (C) pest     (D) passenger

(　　) 16. The junior manager is assigned to sign a contract with a new _____ at 2 p.m. today.

    (A) patient     (B) client     (C) receiver     (D) tourist

(    ) 17. I'm opposed to hunting because it's against my _____ of respecting all living creatures.

    (A) principals     (B) principles     (C) potentials     (D) parachutes

(    ) 18. Don't carry too much cash with you. You can open a(n) _____ account and then save your money in the bank.

    (A) savings     (B) athletes     (C) adjustments     (D) departures

(    ) 19. The student expressed her sincere _____ to the professor for his valuable instruction.

    (A) hammer     (B) gratitude     (C) linen     (D) opera

(    ) 20. The children are watching a caterpillar _____ up the flower stem.

    (A) digging     (B) sneaking     (C) crawling     (D) stretching

## II. Fill in the Blank （從下方選出適合字彙做適當變化，填入答案）

| isolate | long | traffic | response | expose |
| --- | --- | --- | --- | --- |

_____ 1. The child who got the flu had to be _____ from the other healthy children in the family.

_____ 2. The soldiers are _____ to dangers. They are left unprotected.

_____ 3. The government did nothing in _____ to people's complaints about the terrible traffic in the city.

_____ 4. After years of conflict between the two countries, people from both sides are _____ for peace.

_____ 5. There are always _____ jams during rush hour in big cities.

## III. Guided Translation （寫出完整字彙）

1. 你永遠不會相信我在機場遇到了誰。我碰巧遇到你姐姐。

You would never believe whom I r_____ a_____ at the airport. I met your sister by chance.

2. 颱風逼近，戶外演唱會是否能如期舉行還無法確定。

As the typhoon is approaching, it's b_____ n_____ m_____ certain that the outdoor concert will be held as scheduled.

3. 健康食品不應含有合成化學物質。

Health foods are supposed to be f_____ o_____ synthetic chemicals.

4. Jim 在回家的路上，順道去水果攤買了一些蘋果。

Jim stopped by a fruit stand to buy some apples o_____ his w_____ home.

5. Paul 非常高興他的妻子平安地生下一個健康的嬰兒。

Paul was absolutely delighted that his wife g_____ b_____ t_____ a healthy baby safely.

# Round 25

## I. Multiple Choice

(    ) 1. Parents _____ that the authorities should take immediate action to stop the further spread of the virus among children.
   (A) ensure      (B) rule      (C) admit      (D) urge

(    ) 2. The two teams are competing for the gold _____ in the International Mathematical Olympiad.
   (A) medal      (B) cast      (C) necktie      (D) gown

(    ) 3. It is very important to _____ a balance in the natural world so that all living creatures can survive.
   (A) stain      (B) contain      (C) maintain      (D) entertain

(    ) 4. Train 205 will be delayed for 30 minutes, and the station staff _____ for any inconvenience caused.
   (A) consents      (B) apologizes      (C) worries      (D) tumbles

(    ) 5. Don't be _____. How can you expect others to forgive you every time you make a mistake?
   (A) ridiculous      (B) connected      (C) pessimistic      (D) intensive

(    ) 6. Louis wishes to be a swimming _____, teaching people how to swim.
   (A) alcoholic      (B) candidate      (C) circus      (D) instructor

(    ) 7. I think Jay should learn to be _____ about his achievements. There is nothing noble in feeling superior to others.
   (A) confident      (B) humorous      (C) modest      (D) careful

( ) 8. The refugees _____ for support from international aid organizations.

(A) beg      (B) clarify      (C) scoop      (D) plot

( ) 9. That is _____ what Theo said. Actually, I am not very sure about it.

(A) gradually      (B) miserably      (C) slightly      (D) roughly

( ) 10. This coat is made of very _____ material. It will last several years.

(A) joint      (B) durable      (C) mere      (D) political

( ) 11. Owing to the _____ recession, it seems impossible for our company to achieve the objective of a 10% increase in sales.

(A) informative      (B) economic      (C) relative      (D) executive

( ) 12. The professional athlete had gone through all kinds of _____ before he made a name for himself.

(A) casinos      (B) theses      (C) hardships      (D) innings

( ) 13. The company hired several part-timers to hand out free _____ of shampoo on the street.

(A) lectures      (B) temples      (C) napkins      (D) samples

( ) 14. A significant _____ of this robotic vacuum cleaner is its capability of detecting dirty areas of the house.

(A) feature      (B) route      (C) attempt      (D) illustration

( ) 15. We need a _____ to access the classified files on the computer.

(A) pastime      (B) passion      (C) poison      (D) password

( ) 16. The single parent works very hard to feed and _____ his three children.

(A) attribute      (B) clothe      (C) testify      (D) endorse

( ) 17. In court, everyone should have equal rights; no one can enjoy any _____ .

(A) endorsements (B) illusions      (C) privileges      (D) profits

(      ) 18. All people aboard died in the plane crash, including the pilots, passengers, and the _____.

(A) crew      (B) crow      (C) chew      (D) crowd

(      ) 19. Running out of cash, Gary _____ NT$5,000 from the ATM in the convenience store.

(A) deposited      (B) withdrew      (C) disturbed      (D) conceived

(      ) 20. Could you _____ what the robber looked like in detail?

(A) prescribe      (B) distract      (C) describe      (D) assault

## II. Fill in the Blank （從下方選出適合字彙做適當變化，填入答案）

| course | blame | worth | count | gear |
|---|---|---|---|---|

_____ 1. You can always _____ on me when you are in need.

_____ 2. In the awards ceremony, the actress wore a black evening dress with a diamond necklace that was _____ approximately US$150,000.

_____ 3. Those careless campers were _____ for starting the forest fire.

_____ 4. The tourist hotels in Miami Beach are all _____ up for the upcoming holiday season.

_____ 5. In the _____ of the interview, it was gradually clear that this applicant was not qualified for the position.

## III. Guided Translation （寫出完整字彙）

1. James 關掉電視機，不情願地回到自己的房間。

James turned off the TV set and went back to his room u_____ p_____.

2. 經理被工作壓力逼到了極點，然後那天就辭職了。

The manager was driven t_____ e_____ by the pressure from his work, then he quit that day.

3. 聽覺損失的人可以透過手語溝通。

People with hearing loss can communicate b_____ m_____ o_____ sign language.

4. 在登船之前，每位乘客都被要求穿上救生衣以確保安全。

Before boarding the boat, every passenger was asked to put on a life jacket f_____ t_____ s_____ o_____ safety.

5. Justin 怯場了，因為這是他第一次面對如此多的觀眾。

Justin got s_____ f_____ since it was the first time he faced a large audience.

# Round 26

## I. Multiple Choice

(　　) 1. To live a long and healthy life, you must ＿＿＿ greasy food.
　　(A) lag　　　　(B) impose　　(C) hook　　　(D) avoid

(　　) 2. The advertisement misleads consumers by claiming that the ＿＿＿ tea can make them lose 10 pounds within a week.
　　(A) herbal　　(B) absolute　　(C) keen　　　(D) racial

(　　) 3. A large ＿＿＿ of the population favors the recent reforms of the educational system.
　　(A) variety　　(B) majority　　(C) heap　　　(D) sum

(　　) 4. The idea of sleeping in on Sundays is quite ＿＿＿ to the busy career woman.
　　(A) following　　(B) allowing　　(C) appealing　　(D) admiring

(　　) 5. Although the food in the restaurant is expensive, I often have dinner there because of its good ＿＿＿.
　　(A) interference　(B) observation　(C) service　　(D) limitation

(　　) 6. Many scholars and ＿＿＿ gathered in the meeting room, talking about some educational issues.
　　(A) intellectuals　(B) pedestrians　(C) servants　　(D) guardians

(　　) 7. The students are practicing speaking skills with each other, while the teacher is ＿＿＿ their progress.
　　(A) monitoring　(B) suspending　(C) dialing　　(D) criticizing

(　　) 8. If Chloe promise to ＿＿＿ herself in public, her father will take her to the science museum this Saturday.
　　(A) create　　(B) fascinate　　(C) decorate　　(D) behave

(   ) 9. Lacking a _____ of direction, Nancy frequently gets lost when going to a new place.

(A) glory      (B) sense      (C) supervision      (D) glimpse

(   ) 10. Are you in deadly _____ when saying you are going to quit your job?

(A) heart      (B) intention      (C) earnest      (D) tendency

(   ) 11. The boy pulled at the _____ of his mother's blouse, saying he wanted to go to the bathroom.

(A) scarf      (B) cap      (C) chest      (D) sleeve

(   ) 12. Please pour more _____ on the spaghetti. It will be more delicious.

(A) sword      (B) sauce      (C) leather      (D) grace

(   ) 13. Disease is the _____ of humankind.

(A) enemy      (B) publisher      (C) designer      (D) fellow

(   ) 14. The teacher is _____ enough to explain the sentence over and over again until every student understands it.

(A) awful      (B) remote      (C) fierce      (D) patient

(   ) 15. Frank marked his girlfriend's birthday on the _____ in case he might forget.

(A) custom      (B) opera      (C) calendar      (D) history

(   ) 16. At first, cellphones were _____ to carry around, but now they are much slimmer.

(A) clumsy      (B) genuine      (C) suitable      (D) noble

(   ) 17. Applicants must follow the proper _____ for applying for a visa.

(A) promotion      (B) progress      (C) procedure      (D) provision

(   ) 18. The scholar is _____ of the new housing policy. He thinks it will lead to an overheated real estate market.

(A) proud      (B) cruel      (C) ambitious      (D) critical

(     ) 19. The clip from the old newspaper _____ me of the terrible accident that happened in my youth.

    (A) recalled     (B) reminded     (C) remembered   (D) reflected

(     ) 20. The translator did such a good job that she _____ every penny she earned.

    (A) demanded     (B) deserved     (C) desired     (D) deepened

## II. Fill in the Blank （從下方選出適合字彙做適當變化，填入答案）

| memory | season | block | schedule | pluck |
|---|---|---|---|---|

_____ 1. These peaches must be very expensive, for they are out of _____.

_____ 2. The voluntary organization built a monument in _____ of the victims who died during the severe earthquake.

_____ 3. All the roads out of the village were _____ off by the enemy. Thus, the villagers could not obtain any supplies.

_____ 4. Don't be afraid. _____ up the courage to fight against your opponent.

_____ 5. The project took so much time that it was completed several weeks behind _____.

## III. Guided Translation （寫出完整字彙）

1. 當我外出度假時，我的鄰居能照看我的房子真是太好了。

It was nice of my neighbors to k_____ a_____ e_____ o_____ my house when I was away on vacation.

2. 我確定這間咖啡廳接受信用卡，但我還是會帶一些現金，以防萬一。

I'm certain the café takes credit cards, but I still bring some cash with me, just i_____ c_____.

3. 這個小男孩故意弄壞他的玩具，以引起他父母的注意。

The little boy broke his toy o_____ p_____ to attract his parents' attention.

4. 醫院試圖掩蓋醫療錯誤，但沒有成功。這成了頭條新聞。

The hospital tried to c_____ u_____ the medical error, but in vain. It was in the headlines.

5. 這間公司分崩離析，因為前執行長去世，沒有人願意接手。

The company f_____ a_____ because the former CEO passed away, and nobody wanted to take it over.

# Round 27

## I. Multiple Choice

(     ) 1. The computer is a _____ invention. It has changed the way people live.
     (A) conservative   (B) functional    (C) revolutionary   (D) fluent

(     ) 2. I didn't tell Fiona the bad news for fear that she might be _____ about it.
     (A) fresh      (B) organic      (C) upset      (D) handy

(     ) 3. Good time _____ is very important to people who work on a tight schedule.
     (A) judgment      (B) management  (C) advertisement (D) achievement

(     ) 4. I'd like to make a(n) _____ with Dr. Miller this evening, please.
     (A) donor      (B) influence      (C) explanation    (D) appointment

(     ) 5. The talk show host's jokes made the audience _____ with laughter.
     (A) roar      (B) murmur      (C) panic      (D) adapt

(     ) 6. The boy charged with _____ is only sixteen and should go to juvenile court.
     (A) robbery      (B) innovation      (C) stream      (D) swing

(     ) 7. With proper incentives, curiosity can be turned into a strong _____ for learning.
     (A) motivation      (B) quotation      (C) suspicion      (D) invitation

(     ) 8. The player _____ to a tennis club which is very hard to get into.
     (A) confines      (B) belongs      (C) lends      (D) relates

(      ) 9. Doris broke the _____ of her daily life. She went to see a play instead of going to work.

(A) gravity      (B) routine      (C) silence      (D) pitch

(      ) 10. The medicine _____ my pain in five minutes. I'm feeling much better now.

(A) endured      (B) underwent      (C) altered      (D) eased

(      ) 11. You should not run away from the _____ but face them and try to overcome them.

(A) harvests      (B) obstacles      (C) goods      (D) ingredients

(      ) 12. Some environmentalists will lead a(n) _____ against the use of plastic straws this Sunday.

(A) notion      (B) investment      (C) negotiation      (D) campaign

(      ) 13. A _____ was sent out to rescue two injured people in the mountains.

(A) heater      (B) date      (C) helicopter      (D) sector

(      ) 14. The _____ author has published more than ten crime novels during the past five years.

(A) productive      (B) rigid      (C) noticeable      (D) sentimental

(      ) 15. Remember to wear a _____ to protect your head when riding on a motorcycle.

(A) handle      (B) hut      (C) helmet      (D) heritage

(      ) 16. The main _____ grown in the area for export are coffee and cotton.

(A) muscles      (B) particles      (C) crops      (D) vehicles

(      ) 17. Susan doesn't want to get married. She wants to remain _____ for her entire life.

(A) single      (B) anonymous      (C) intact      (D) isolated

(     ) 18. The villagers made a(n) _____ attempt to stop the construction of the dam.

      (A) fundamental   (B) prevailing    (C) ethnic      (D) desperate

(     ) 19. The main duty of an astronomer is to _____ the stars in space.

      (A) endanger     (B) concede    (C) follow     (D) observe

(     ) 20. Ray is a patriotic _____ who is always ready to defend his country.

      (A) cinema      (B) citizen     (C) clay     (D) constant

## II. Fill in the Blank（從下方選出適合字彙做適當變化，填入答案）

| scene | book | presence | fall | pour |
|---|---|---|---|---|

_____ 1. My brother _____ cold water on my idea by saying that it wouldn't work at all.

_____ 2. The two CEOs drew up the plan to merge the two businesses into one behind the _____ rather than in public.

_____ 3. Marian felt very embarrassed as her joke _____ flat. No one laughed at it.

_____ 4. The drawing of the lottery was held in the _____ of all the parents who intended to enroll their children in the school.

_____ 5. To our disappointment, the hotel has been fully _____ up during the long weekend.

## III. Guided Translation（寫出完整字彙）

1. 那個搖滾樂團很受年輕人歡迎，尤其女孩子們被英俊的主唱所吸引。

The rock band is popular with young people, and girls, i_____ p_____, are attracted to the handsome vocalist.

2. 傳單被風吹走了，所以工讀生在街上追著它們跑。

The leaflets were b_____ a_____, so the part-timer ran after them on the street.

3. Tanya 取笑 George 因為他穿了雙古怪的靴子。

   Tanya m_____ f_____ o_____ George

   because he wore a pair of strange boots.

4. 你一到火車站就打給我。我會過去接你。

   Call me a_____ s_____ a_____ you arrive at

   the train station. I'll go to pick you up.

5. 我工作忙得精疲力盡。如果不趕快放個假,我想我就要發瘋了。

   I'm exhausted from my busy work. I think I'll g_____

   c_____ if I don't take a vacation soon.

# Round 28

## I. Multiple Choice

(      ) 1. To protect itself from the predator, the butterfly _____ blended in with its surroundings.

   (A) swiftly      (B) productively   (C) apparently      (D) sensitively

(      ) 2. The miners' tools are still _____, so it is hard to increase their production.

   (A) advanced      (B) splendid      (C) primitive      (D) technological

(      ) 3. Table _____ vary from culture to culture, so it is advisable to follow the examples of local people.

   (A) manners      (B) menus      (C) methods      (D) measures

(      ) 4. Lunchtime is _____, so let's go get something to eat.

   (A) instituting      (B) approaching   (C) resembling      (D) consuming

(      ) 5. It was cruel that a lot of infants and children were _____ from their parents during the war.

   (A) frustrated      (B) calculated      (C) declared      (D) separated

(      ) 6. Before every flight takes off, it has to undergo a detailed safety _____.

   (A) infection      (B) injection      (C) inspection      (D) institution

(      ) 7. The Queen has a substantial collection of _____ jewelry, which have been passed down from generation to generation.

   (A) partial      (B) compound      (C) progressive   (D) antique

(      ) 8. I think I have _____ greatly from your valuable advice.

   (A) damaged      (B) educated      (C) emphasized   (D) benefited

( ) 9. Mr. Black gained great _____ from the success of his project.

   (A) transaction    (B) satisfaction    (C) migration    (D) election

( ) 10. The earthquake victims couldn't help crying upon seeing the _____ from their collapsed houses.

   (A) athletics    (B) debris    (C) compliance    (D) citizenship

( ) 11. Generally speaking, an immigrant must pass a test to _____ American citizenship.

   (A) retain    (B) acquire    (C) sustain    (D) grant

( ) 12. The school starts its new teaching programs with the _____ that no child is left behind.

   (A) prescription    (B) compromise    (C) premise    (D) consumption

( ) 13. The diplomat promised to _____ the problem. He was confident that he could make a satisfactory arrangement.

   (A) contribute    (B) settle    (C) exaggerate    (D) import

( ) 14. *Frankenstein*, which was written by Mary Shelley, is considered to be the first work of science _____.

   (A) fiction    (B) essay    (C) romance    (D) album

( ) 15. If I have a _____ afternoon all by myself, I will read novels and listen to soft music.

   (A) shocking    (B) frightening    (C) chilly    (D) peaceful

( ) 16. If you don't know the _____ of the department, you can call the operator and have your call transferred.

   (A) extension    (B) persuasion    (C) protection    (D) solution

( ) 17. Anita is allergic to dairy _____ and has to eliminate them from her diet.

   (A) purposes    (B) puzzles    (C) promises    (D) products

(     ) 18. Jerry's parents made enormous _____ to give him a better education. They worked hard to afford his tuition.
     (A) energies      (B) temptations      (C) sacrifices      (D) frustrations

(     ) 19. _____ the fact that there was little hope of finding anyone alive, the search still went on.
     (A) Unless      (B) Lest      (C) Despite      (D) Concerning

(     ) 20. The survey revealed the gender pay gap in the 1970s. Men and women were not treated equally in the _____.
     (A) workplace      (B) lobby      (C) backyard      (D) corridor

## II. Fill in the Blank （從下方選出適合字彙做適當變化，填入答案）

| possession | fail | bottom | credit | notice |
|---|---|---|---|---|

_____ 1. While going through customs, the man was found in _____ of drugs and was arrested on the spot.

_____ 2. Since the couple didn't have enough money on hand, they decided to pay for the car on _____.

_____ 3. It's impossible for us to make arrangements for such a big dinner party on short _____.

_____ 4. Extra information about this smartphone model will be found at the _____ of the web page.

_____ 5. A lack of teamwork proved fatal to the project. It _____ in the end.

## III. Guided Translation （寫出完整字彙）

1. 令我驚訝的是，我迷戀的那個女孩沒事先通知我，就來了我的生日派對。

     T_____ m_____ s_____, the girl I had a crush on came to my birthday party without informing me in advance.

2. Johnny 的爸爸把同樣的床邊故事說了一遍又一遍,讓他覺得很無聊。

Johnny got bored because his father repeated the same bedtime story

o_____ a_____ o_____.

3. 洞穴裡曾經有海盜於 17 世紀埋藏的寶藏。

There u_____ t_____ b_____ treasures

buried in the cave by the pirates in the 17th century.

4. 那場考試根本不簡單。我只答得出一半的題目。

The test was f_____ f_____ easy. I could only answer

half of the questions.

5. 無庸置疑地是你不努力工作的話什麼也得不到。

It g_____ w_____ s_____ that you get

nothing without hard work.

# Round 29

## I. Multiple Choice

(　　) 1. Mr. and Mrs. James were moved to tears when seeing their son receiving a _____ at the graduation ceremony.
(A) ladder　　(B) diploma　　(C) surveillance　(D) counter

(　　) 2. When we asked Prof. Wang about the current economic situation, he was quite reserved and didn't want to make any _____.
(A) comments　(B) occupations　(C) spades　　(D) tortoises

(　　) 3. The two teams will a have volleyball game in the _____ tomorrow.
(A) wreck　　(B) gallery　　(C) gymnasium　(D) court

(　　) 4. Most people think the _____ should take responsibility for the collapse of the building.
(A) adventure　(B) advertise　(C) architect　(D) screw

(　　) 5. The lifeguard took the _____ of losing his own life to save the drowning boy.
(A) defense　　(B) location　　(C) exposure　　(D) risk

(　　) 6. Don't take Michael's words _____. He often speaks with no concern for others.
(A) seriously　(B) lately　　(C) lightly　　(D) legally

(　　) 7. The performer tried to hide his nervousness, but instead he made it even more _____.
(A) original　　(B) obvious　　(C) delicate　　(D) individual

(　　) 8. Tomorrow's football match is _____ owing to the typhoon. Tickets will be refunded.
(A) executed　(B) canceled　　(C) disappeared　(D) transited

(    ) 9. Phoebe _____ me by screaming abruptly behind my back.

     (A) orbited      (B) repaired      (C) forbidden      (D) scared

(    ) 10. It was so dark that I couldn't recognize the tall _____ in the dark.

     (A) field      (B) fight      (C) fence      (D) figure

(    ) 11. There is a _____ smell in the house. It makes me feel sick.

     (A) plentiful      (B) gracious      (C) holy      (D) peculiar

(    ) 12. People can taste various _____ flavors of food such as Thai, Italian, and Japanese cuisine in the night market.

     (A) clinical      (B) exotic      (C) harsh      (D) graphic

(    ) 13. _____ has it that war will break out soon, so many people are fleeing to other countries.

     (A) Trend      (B) Convention      (C) Rumor      (D) Chance

(    ) 14. Since you are a beginner, I'll give you some tips on how to _____ money in stocks.

     (A) bid      (B) invest      (C) bounce      (D) accord

(    ) 15. Nowadays, quite a few young people want to enter the legal _____. They believe being a lawyer is a profitable job.

     (A) version      (B) transmission      (C) profession      (D) preservation

(    ) 16. The _____ between the East and the West are greatly different such as beliefs and customs.

     (A) cultures      (B) cues      (C) curls      (D) cushions

(    ) 17. Mina is going to meet her former husband to _____ their daughter's health problems.

     (A) cope      (B) remain      (C) discuss      (D) reverse

(    ) 18. The _____ in our town tracked down the killer, who had murdered over 20 people, and finally solved the case.

     (A) founder      (B) shepherd      (C) ancestor      (D) sheriff

(     ) 19. Tommy was disappointed when Eva _____ his invitation to a romance dinner.

     (A) refused      (B) rebelled      (C) disagreed      (D) disapproved

(     ) 20. It goes without saying that I will get there earlier than you. Let's _____ on that.

     (A) bet      (B) rely      (C) focus      (D) count

## II. Fill in the Blank（從下方選出適合字彙做適當變化，填入答案）

| consequence | cheat | lead | deal | cure |
|---|---|---|---|---|

_____ 1. Don't listen to the man. He is as cunning as a fox and is very likely to _____ you.

_____ 2. With proper treatment, the patient was finally _____ of lung cancer a year later.

_____ 3. The director's next film will _____ with the relationship between a woman and her unfaithful husband.

_____ 4. Throughout the race, Steve was taking the _____, and no one was able to catch up with him.

_____ 5. Samuel has to take the _____ of his actions.

## III. Guided Translation（寫出完整字彙）

1. 公車上太擠以至於幾乎不可能挪出空間來再容納一個人。

The bus is so crowded that it is n_____ t_____ i_____ to make room for one more person.

2. 那個被寵壞的孩子總是認為父母事事幫他做好、對他有求必應，這些都是理所當然的。

The spoiled child always t_____ it f_____ g_____ that his parents should do everything for him and give him everything he asks for.

3. 車子在我們上班的途中拋錨；因此，我們今天都遲到了。

The car b_____ d_____ on our way to work; thus, we were all late today.

4. 那位老先生在搖滾演唱會上和一大群年輕人站在一起時，感覺自己格格不入。

The old man felt o_____ o_____ p_____ while standing with a large crowd of young people at the rock concert.

5. 執行長透過在全國各地開設數百間連鎖店，推動公司的擴張。

The CEO b_____ a_____ his company's expansion by setting up hundreds of chain stores throughout the country.

# Round 30

## I. Multiple Choice

(　　) 1. Ed and Mia tend to be nasty to those who hold different _____ from them. Thus, they often get into fights.

    (A) illusions　　(B) associations　(C) combinations　(D) opinions

(　　) 2. At 11 p.m., the boy was _____ to go back to his bedroom at his mother's request.

    (A) reluctant　　(B) fortunate　　(C) attractive　　(D) generous

(　　) 3. The _____ of the coffeehouse chain is in Taipei, while its branches are all over Taiwan.

    (A) exteriors　　(B) trumpets　　(C) shelters　　(D) headquarters

(　　) 4. The writer's latest book has so far _____ little interest of the public.

    (A) arisen　　(B) risen　　(C) aroused　　(D) raised

(　　) 5. Luckily, with the car mechanic's help, Isaac's minivan finally came to life, and he could _____ his trip.

    (A) bully　　(B) continue　　(C) horrify　　(D) indicate

(　　) 6. As the number of cars has _____, there is much more traffic on roads in recent years.

    (A) mushroomed　(B) declined　　(C) articulated　　(D) divided

(　　) 7. I've got nothing to tell you _____ what I have already said.

    (A) beyond　　(B) beneath　　(C) below　　(D) behind

(　　) 8. Alishan is famous for its beautiful _____, especially the magnificent sunrise. No wonder it attracts a large number of tourists.

    (A) scenery　　(B) publicity　　(C) volume　　(D) definition

(　) 9. The library is very quiet, with only _____ coughs from the students there.
(A) terminal　　(B) authentic　　(C) occasional　　(D) essential

(　) 10. To reduce global _____ dioxide emissions, we have to focus on two fundamental areas: energy and agriculture.
(A) canyon　　(B) canoe　　(C) carbon　　(D) canvas

(　) 11. I need a pair of _____ to cut the string. Could you fetch it for me?
(A) stockings　　(B) scissors　　(C) socks　　(D) pants

(　) 12. Nick has learned a lesson after the unfortunate incident, _____ that a friend in need is a friend indeed.
(A) undoubtedly　　(B) scarcely　　(C) namely　　(D) presumably

(　) 13. Working in the garden, Jessica noticed a strange man _____ into her neighbor's house.
(A) substituting　　(B) peeping　　(C) fainting　　(D) hesitating

(　) 14. I'm burning with _____. Please tell me who won the game at last.
(A) sensitivity　　(B) flexibility　　(C) credibility　　(D) curiosity

(　) 15. Our restaurant has just managed to survive; we don't know when it will become _____.
(A) indispensable　(B) profitable　　(C) beneficial　　(D) financial

(　) 16. Grace is pursuing her life goal with _____. Thus, we believe she will succeed someday.
(A) determination　(B) integration　　(C) presidency　　(D) agency

(　) 17. Malala is _____ to fighting for the rights to free and complete education for girls and young women.
(A) donated　　(B) selected　　(C) departed　　(D) devoted

(　) 18. We should _____ our heads when an emergency arises.
(A) hang　　(B) lose　　(C) strike　　(D) keep

(    ) 19. During the period of Imperial China, the dragon was generally _____ with great power.

(A) accompanied    (B) associated     (C) conformed     (D) rhymed

(    ) 20. The landslide caused by the _____ typhoon killed dozens of people and left many more homeless.

(A) urgent        (B) dependent     (C) violent      (D) intelligent

## II. Fill in the Blank （從下方選出適合字彙做適當變化，填入答案）

| injure | degree | solve | search | brush |
|--------|--------|-------|--------|-------|

_____ 1. Alfred took pains to _____ math problems in the hope of getting good grades.

_____ 2. Before you go to Germany, I suggest you _____ up your German. Then, it will be easier for you to communicate with the locals.

_____ 3. The police _____ the whole area for the missing woman, but they still found no clue.

_____ 4. Hard work made the worker's financial status improve by _____.

_____ 5. The police officer wears a jacket which is resistant to bullets so that she won't get _____ in a shoot-out.

## III. Guided Translation （寫出完整字彙）

1. 走了兩個小時之後，我現在想喝杯冰水想喝得要死。

After a two-hour walk, I'm d_____ f_____ a glass of iced water now.

2. 理所當然地，如果你不準時繳交房租就會被趕出去。

It s＿＿＿＿＿＿ t＿＿＿＿＿＿ r＿＿＿＿＿＿ that you will be thrown out if you don't pay the rent on time.

3. 在簽約之前，你得要確認運費是否包含在價錢中。

Before signing the contract, you have to make sure whether the shipping fee is b＿＿＿＿＿ i＿＿＿＿＿ the price or not.

4. Lopez 小姐無意下廚，所以她經常外食。

Ms. Lopez has no intention of cooking, so she usually d＿＿＿＿＿＿ o＿＿＿＿＿＿.

5. 那些登山客被暴風雨困住時，躲在一個山洞裡避難。

The hikers t＿＿＿＿＿＿ r＿＿＿＿＿＿ in a cave when they were caught in a storm.

# 神拿滿級分——英文學測總複習(二版)

孫至娟　編著

- 重點搭配練習：雙效合一有感複習，讓你應試力 UP ！

- 議題式心智圖：補充時事議題單字，讓你單字力 UP ！

- 文章主題多元：符合學測多元取材，讓你閱讀力 UP ！

- 混合題最素養：多樣混合題型訓練，讓你理解力 UP ！

- 獨立作文頁面：作答空間超好運用，讓你寫作力 UP ！

- 詳盡解析考點：見題拆題精闢解析，讓你解題力 UP ！

# 核心英文字彙力
## 2001～4500(三版)

丁雍嫻 邢雯桂
盧思嘉 應惠蕙　編著

◆依據大學入學考試中心公布之「高中英文參考詞彙表
(111 學年度起適用)」編寫，一起迎戰 108 新課綱。
單字比對歷屆試題，依字頻平均分散各回。

◆收錄 Level 3~5 學測必備單字，規劃 100 回。
聚焦關鍵核心字彙、備戰學測。
Level 3：40 回
Level 4：40 回
Level 5-1( 精選 Level 5 高頻單字 )：20 回

◆精心撰寫各式情境例句，符合 108 新課綱素養精神。
除了可以利用例句學習單字用法、加深單字記憶，更
能熟悉學測常見情境、為大考做好準備。

◆常用搭配詞、介系詞、同反義字及片語等各項補充豐富，
一起舉一反三、輕鬆延伸學習範圍。

國家圖書館出版品預行編目資料

30天計畫：打造核心英文字彙題本／丁雍嫻,邢雯桂,
盧思嘉,應惠蕙編著.－－初版一刷.－－臺北市：三
民，2023
　　　面；　　公分.－－（英語Make Me High系列）

　　ISBN 978－957－14－7643－8　（平裝）
　　1. 英語 2. 詞彙

805.12　　　　　　　　　　　　　　　　112007041

英 *Make Me High* 系列
語

# 30 天計畫：打造核心英文字彙題本

| | |
|---|---|
| 編 著 者 | 丁雍嫻　邢雯桂　盧思嘉　應惠蕙 |
| 責任編輯 | 劉虹慧 |
| 發 行 人 | 劉振強 |
| 出 版 者 | 三民書局股份有限公司 |
| 地　　址 | 臺北市復興北路 386 號 ( 復北門市 ) |
| | 臺北市重慶南路一段 61 號 ( 重南門市 ) |
| 電　　話 | (02)25006600 |
| 網　　址 | 三民網路書店 https://www.sanmin.com.tw |
| 出版日期 | 初版一刷 2023 年 6 月 |
| 書籍編號 | S872390 |
| I S B N | 978-957-14-7643-8 |

三民書局

108課綱、全民英檢中級適用

英語 *Make Me High* 系列

# 30天計畫：
## 打造 核心 英文字彙題本

解析本

丁雍嫻 邢雯桂 盧思嘉 應惠蕙 編著

Every Day Matters

—— 備戰 30 天 ——

全面掌握核心字彙

4500

三民書局

# Table of Contents

檢討完一個回次後，你可以在該回次的⊘打勾並在 12/31 填寫完成日期。

# Round 1

## I. Multiple Choice

| 1. A | 2. D | 3. A | 4. A | 5. B |
|------|------|------|------|------|
| 6. B | 7. C | 8. A | 9. D | 10. C |
| 11. D | 12. B | 13. D | 14. B | 15. D |
| 16. A | 17. B | 18. C | 19. C | 20. C |

1. Lena 嘗試在她的小狗窒息時救牠，但不幸的是，牠仍失去了生命。
   (A) **窒息**；(B) 完成；(C) 使破產；(D) 面臨

2. 這名市長宣布支持改革以反駁來自政府官員們的批評。
   (A) 汙染；(B) 包紮；(C) 延長；**(D) 反駁**

3. 孩子們在美術課上畫畫需要幾張紙。
   **(A) 張 (紙)**；(B) 條 (麵包)；(C) 薄片；(D) 罐子

4. 研究指出，這種疾病是由缺陷基因引起而非細菌。
   **(A) 基因**；(B) 出生；(C) 設計；(D) 媒介

5. 遊輪撞上冰山後迅速下沉，因此船長下令棄船。
   (A) 透露；**(B) 拋棄**；(C) 溺死；(D) 吸收

6. 遊客們感到心煩，因為暴風雨毀了他們在熱帶島嶼上的假期。
   (A) 避免；**(B) 毀掉**；(C) 旋轉；(D) 潑濺

7. 手術後，病人的傷口沒過多久就痊癒了。
   (A) 治療；(B) 商量；**(C) 癒合**；(D) 感染

8. Ben 的房子被闖入後，警方請他列出遺失物品清單。
   **(A) 物件**；(B) 事情；(C) 事件；(D) 圓圈

9. 男孩沒有報復曾經欺負他的人，而是決定原諒與寬恕。
   (A) 加強；(B) 修訂；(C) 審查；**(D) 報復**

10. 該公司原先預期會有數百名求職者。然而，只有幾個人申請了這個職位。
    (A) 徹底改變；(B) 決定；**(C) 預期**；(D) 證明

11. 幸福的婚姻必須建立在夫妻之間相互尊重和理解的基礎上。
    (A) 常見的；(B) 雙人的；(C) 學術的；**(D) 互相的**

12. 那名顧客用一百美元的鈔票支付她的餐費。
    (A) 紙；**(B) 鈔票**；(C) 銀行；(D) 藥丸

13. 空氣中瀰漫著鹽味，說明大海就在不遠處。
    (A) 主張；(B) 談論；(C) 命令；**(D) 暗示**

14. 情緒失控的 Chloe 無法專注於她正在做的任何事情，並一直想著痛苦的分手。
    (A) 通常地；**(B) 情感地**；(C) 邏輯地；(D) 直率地

15. 任何帶有性別或種族歧視含義的言語都會被認為是冒犯的。
    (A) 教育的；(B) 破壞性的；(C) 恭敬的；**(D) 冒犯的**

16. 這座新建的棒球場有五萬個座位。
    **(A) 容量**；(B) 預定；(C) 責任；(D) 悲劇

17. 如今，越來越多人沉迷於智慧型手機。一些人就是不能沒有他們。
    (A) 脆弱的；**(B) 使沉迷**；(C) 令人嚮往的；(D) 擔心的

18. 這個山區仍缺乏足夠的醫療設施。
    (A) 構成；(B) 慈善事業；**(C) 設施**；(D) 邊界

19. 年輕人傾向與同儕分享他們的祕密而不是父母。
    (A) 學生；(B) 火柴；**(C) 同儕**；(D) 公司

20. 這名時裝設計師每月為流行雜誌撰寫當前流行趨勢的專欄。
    (A) 殖民地；(B) 密碼；**(C) 專欄**；(D) 複印

## II. Fill in the Blank

| 1. account | 2. disguise | 3. length |
|------------|-------------|-----------|
| 4. burnt/burned | 5. absence | |

1. 我希望我的老闆會考慮到我做簡報時是生病的。★ take sth into account 把某事列入考慮

2. 錯過我的班機是因禍得福，因為飛機剛起飛就墜毀了。★ a blessing in disguise 因禍得福

3. 這位水手詳盡地講述了他在海上的冒險故事和瀕臨死亡的經驗。★ at length 詳盡地

4. 戰爭結束後，災民回來發現他們的房子已經被燒毀。★ burn (sth) down 燒毀，焚毀

5. 在沒有其他更好的應徵者情況下，我們決定將這份工作提供給 Baker 先生。
   ★ in the absence of 缺少

## III. Guided Translation

1. lay; off
2. No; sooner; than
3. is; used; to
4. got; away
5. left; behind

# Round 2

## I. Multiple Choice

| | | | | |
|---|---|---|---|---|
| 1. A | 2. A | 3. D | 4. C | 5. B |
| 6. D | 7. B | 8. A | 9. D | 10. A |
| 11. D | 12. C | 13. A | 14. C | 15. B |
| 16. C | 17. B | 18. B | 19. C | 20. D |

1. 豔陽融化我的冰淇淋，讓我的手黏答答的。
   (A) **黏答答的**；(B) 多岩石的；(C) 熱烈的；(D) 巨大的

2. 這種罕見的疾病削弱了 Helen 的免疫系統，使她的身體變得脆弱。
   (A) **嚴重削弱**；(B) 引起；(C) 指引；(D) 畫素描

3. 這名商人對貧窮人非常慷慨。他經常捐款給慈善機構。
   (A) 吝嗇的；(B) 隨機的；(C) 願意的；(D) **慷慨的**

4. 派對結束後，用過的盤子和玻璃杯散落在桌上和地板。收拾髒亂會需要幾個小時。
   (A) 殺；(B) 違抗；(C) **(東西) 被平放**；(D) 築壩

5. 教師應該熟悉各種教學技巧和材料。
   (A) 計算；(B) **技巧**；(C) 知覺；(D) 預報

6. 令我們驚訝的是，經理並沒有暗示他想辭去工作。
   (A) 墨水；(B) 懷疑；(C) 提議；(D) **暗示**

7. 掌握閱讀和寫作技巧需要不斷練習。
   (A) (大量) 生產；(B) **掌握**；(C) 微波；(D) 主修

8. 真皮製成的靴子比人造皮革製成的靴子貴得多。
   (A) **人工的**；(B) 自然的；(C) 藝術的；(D) 令人難忘的

9. 學生們興奮得坐不住了。
   (A) 不利的；(B) 開明的；(C) 深的；(D) **不動的**

10. 當您進入電影院時，一定要知道最近的緊急出口在哪裡。
    (A) **緊急情況**；(B) 擁抱；(C) 帝國；(D) 大使館

11. 神秘的是船隻和飛機在百慕達三角消失得無影無蹤是個謎。
    (A) 精密的；(B) 多話的；(C) 必然的；(D) **神祕的**

12. 我受不了那裡嚴寒的天氣。溫度通常低於攝氏 5 度。
    (A) 晴朗的；(B) 暖和的；(C) **嚴寒的**；(D) 有活力的

13. 這名軟體工程師因為他龐大的工作量而感到壓力很大。
    (A) **壓力**；(B) 資訊；(C) 調查；(D) 國籍

14. 糖醋排骨是這家中式餐廳的招牌菜之一。
    (A) 拖鞋；(B) 幫浦；(C) **招牌菜**；(D) 廚餘

15. 這位導演以他的恐怖片聞名，但他最新的一部是喜劇片。
    (A) 能力；(B) **喜劇**；(C) 電池；(D) (政府的) 部

16. Bill 在高中時的學業成績很好，因此他獲得了大學的獎學金。
    (A) 出身背景；(B) 申請；(C) **獎學金**；(D) 發行量

17. 這些槍支和炸彈純粹是防禦性武器。它們的火力不足以進行全面入侵。
    (A) 圓形的；(B) **防禦性的**；(C) 象牙色的；(D) 模稜兩可的

18. 有人要烤牛肉嗎？我剛把它從烤箱裡拿出來。
    (A) 誠實的；(B) **烘烤的**；(C) 溼潤的；(D) 廣大的

19. 空服員站在登機口迎接乘客登機。
    (A) 去 (在) 國外；(B) 寬的；(C) **上 (火車、船和飛機等)**；(D) (使) 上 (船、火車或飛機等)

20. 運動鞋的銷量飆升是因為運動已經成為人們日常生活重要的一部分。
    (A) 加香料於…；(B) 摻少量的酒、毒藥等；(C) 概述；(D) **暴增**

## II. Fill in the Blank

| | | |
|---|---|---|
| 1. dispute | 2. burst | 3. action |
| 4. sticks | 5. distinguish | |

1. Tyler 夫婦經常在孩子的教育問題上起爭執。
   ★ dispute 起爭執

2. Tim 的笑話太有趣了以至於每個人都突然放聲大笑。★ burst out 突然開始 (做某事)

3. 我相信是時候將計畫付諸行動了。
★ put sth into action 付諸行動

4. Claire 缺乏耐心。她很少堅持任何事情很久。
★ stick to sth 堅持做某事

5. 我的父母教會我如何辨別是非。
★ distinguish 辨別

## III. Guided Translation

1. sooner; or; later
2. come; to; life
3. make; good; use; of
4. get; over
5. as; long; as

# Round 3

## I. Multiple Choice

| | | | | |
|---|---|---|---|---|
| 1. B | 2. B | 3. C | 4. A | 5. D |
| 6. D | 7. C | 8. D | 9. B | 10. C |
| 11. D | 12. A | 13. A | 14. B | 15. C |
| 16. A | 17. B | 18. C | 19. D | 20. A |

1. 你看過我弟弟擺誇張姿勢的搞笑照片嗎？
(A) 形象；(B) **擺姿勢**；(C) 細節；(D) 名譽

2. Jone 一家的房子空蕩蕩的，沒有任何家具，因為他們要搬進更大的房子。
(A) 頻繁的；(B) **空的**；(C) 擺脫掉；(D) 緊張的

3. Louis 是個糟糕的旅伴，因為他總是在抱怨。
(A) 口音；(B) 簽證；(C) **夥伴**；(D) 航空公司

4. 你的想法太抽象，很難理解。你能給我們舉一些具體的例子嗎？
(A) **抽象的**；(B) 適合的；(C) 絕種的；(D) 安排有序的

5. 大多數國際公司會聘請當地律師提供法律意見。
(A) 受訪者；(B) 企業家；(C) 股東；(D) **律師**

6. 我有些猶豫是否要同意這個計畫。我擔心這可能不切實際。
(A) 抱怨；(B) 貪汙腐敗；(C) 革命；(D) **猶豫**

7. 比起同齡人，這個小女孩相當體貼和成熟。
(A) 奇怪的；(B) 使惱怒的；(C) **成熟的**；(D) 骯髒惡臭的

8. Adam 說了這樣的謊應該為自己感到羞愧。
(A) 合作的；(B) 無法抗拒的；(C) 負責的；(D) **羞愧的**

9. 我不喜歡參加社交活動。我不習慣面對陌生人。
(A) 臉部的；(B) **社交的**；(C) 有創造力的；(D) 可靠的

10. 那位作者的第一部小說出版後廣受歡迎。
(A) 不果斷地；(B) 殘忍地；(C) **立即地**；(D) 口頭地

11. 在餐桌上，你應該用餐巾而不是用手擦嘴。
(A) 茶托；(B) 項鍊；(C) 長筒襪；(D) **餐巾**

12. 每當我看到複雜的數學題，腦袋就會一片空白。
(A) **空白的**；(B) 失明的；(C) 錯誤的；(D) 酸的

13. 在臺灣，中秋節吃月餅是一項傳統。
(A) **傳統**；(B) 發明；(C) 學費；(D) 決心

14. 這名罪犯聽了宣判時面無表情。沒有人知道她對此作何感想。
(A) 高興；(B) **情緒**；(C) 因素；(D) 限制

15. 救援行動進行得相當順利。最終，所有乘客和船員都從沉沒的船中獲救。
(A) 一份；(B) 分類；(C) **行動**；(D) 科技

16. 人們可能因非法捕獲石虎和臺灣黑熊等野生動物而被罰款甚至入獄。
(A) **捕獲**；(B) 回應；(C) 合作；(D) 部署

17. Chloe 認為喝湯時發出聲音是不禮貌的。
(A) 圖像；(B) **聲音**；(C) 承諾；(D) 決定

18. 可惜的是當地政府太窮，無力資助這項研究計畫。
(A) 克服；(B) 迫使；(C) **提供資金**；(D) 下載

19. 隨著失業率不斷上升，該城市有很大一部分人找不到工作。
(A) 哲學；(B) 肖像；(C) 優先事項；(D) **百分比**

20. 一艘油輪擱淺在阿拉斯加的一個礁石上，數百萬噸的石油正在洩漏到威廉王子灣。
(A) **(液體或氣體) 漏出**；(B) 把…湊在一起；(C) 跳躍；(D) 分層放置

## II. Fill in the Blank

| | | |
|---|---|---|
| 1. lean | 2. cake | 3. trembling |
| 4. distributed | 5. advance | |

30 天計畫：打造核心英文字彙題本　**解析本**

1. 每次遇到問題，你都可以依靠我。
   ★ lean on sb/sth 依靠…

2. 對於聰明的學生來說，解這道數學問題很簡單。★ a piece of cake 非常容易的事情

3. Zoe 在演講之前，她太緊張以至於忍不住發抖。
   ★ tremble 發抖，顫抖

4. 在開學第一天，這些教科書將被分發給所有新生。★ distribute 分發

5. 如果你要去參加化裝舞會，請事先通知我。
   ★ in advance 事先，提前

### III. Guided Translation

1. In; addition; to
2. as; usual
3. make; up; for
4. by; and; large
5. bit; lip

# Round 4

## I. Multiple Choice

| 1. C | 2. A | 3. C | 4. B | 5. D |
|------|------|------|------|------|
| 6. A | 7. B | 8. C | 9. A | 10. C |
| 11. D | 12. D | 13. A | 14. B | 15. B |
| 16. D | 17. B | 18. A | 19. C | 20. D |

1. 這個國家對於酒駕的處罰有可能是入獄好幾年。
   (A) 反對；(B)安裝；**(C) 處罰**；(D) 獎勵

2. 一臺計程車最多可載四名乘客。現在我們有六個人，我們需要兩臺計程車。
   **(A) 最大限度**；(B) 礦物；(C) 雜誌；(D) 最小限度

3. 中央山脈南北綿延數百公里。
   (A) 阻止；(B) 反應；**(C) 伸展**；(D) 計數

4. 成功沒有神奇的方法。成功屬於努力的人。
   (A) 收據；**(B) 方法**；(C) 轉彎；(D) 首次亮相

5. 許多注重體重的人在進餐時吃瘦肉而不是肥肉。
   (A) 輕微的；(B) 修長的；(C) 苗條的；**(D) (肉) 瘦的**

6. 這部電視劇精確地反映了紐約市的生活和人際關係。

   (A) **精確的**；(B) 有效率的；(C) 官方的；(D) 激烈的

7. 新聞所說的並不總是對真實情況的公正陳述。
   (A) 樂器；**(B) 陳述**；(C) 移動；(D) 實驗

8. 許多人在觀看電影聽到槍聲時，驚恐地尖叫起來。
   (A) 後悔；(B) 失望；**(C) 恐懼**；(D) 開心

9. Maggie 和她家人成功組裝了一個巨大的船艦模型。
   **(A) 組裝**；(B) 向…保證；(C) 假設；(D) 宣稱

10. 令人遺憾的是，病患在手術後不久就因嚴重感染死亡。
    (A) 非常；(B) 普通地；**(C) 不久**；(D) 極其

11. Oliver 的收入低於平均水平，所以他買不起奢侈品。
    (A) 評估；(B) 級別；(C) 比率；**(D) 收入**

12. 煮晚餐時，Matilda 不小心割傷手指，流了很多血。
    (A) 使急速；(B) 逃跑；(C) 流動；**(D) 流血**

13. 共享經濟其實有利於環境。它有助於更加利用閒置資產。
    **(A) 共用**；(B) 占領；(C) 閃光；(D) 激怒

14. 我的英文老師非常重視手寫作業和口語練習。
    (A) 語調；**(B) 重視**；(C) 指導；(D) 尺寸

15. 那個線上購物網站將會大特價。我不會錯過撿些便宜貨的機會。
    (A) 好處；**(B) 機會**；(C) 益處；(D) 註冊

16. 遊客在樹幹上刻上自己的名字是不恰當的。
    (A) 擦掉；(B) 安排；(C) 使敬畏；**(D) 雕刻**

17. 這位演員對無家可歸的孩子感到同情，並捐了一些錢來幫助他們。
    (A) 尷尬；**(B) 同情**；(C) 命運；(D) 憂鬱

18. 那名司機因在高速公路上超速而被重罰。
    **(A) 罰款**；(B) 擊敗；(C) 緩慢行進；(D) 催促

19. 此為私有土地。未經許可人員不得入內。
    (A) 拍賣；(B) 描述；**(C) 許可**；(D) 行列

20. 這位藝術家具有創作天賦。他的原創作品讓所有看過他展覽的人印象深刻。
    (A) 看得見的；(B) 感到懷疑的；(C) 忠誠的；**(D) 有天賦的**

## II. Fill in the Blank

| | | |
|---|---|---|
| 1. vain | 2. lengths | 3. starving |
| 4. drawing | 5. advantage | |

1. 我們的努力是徒勞的，因為這些方法都沒有用。★ in vain 徒勞地，無用地

2. 有些人竭盡全力保持完美身材。
   ★ go to great lengths to V 竭盡全力做

3. 我餓扁了。我們去小吃店吃點東西吧。
   ★ starve (使) 挨餓

4. 女主人正在草擬茶會的賓客名單。
   ★ draw sth up 草擬

5. 我們應該趁著百貨公司的週年慶買些衣服。
   ★ take advantage of sth 利用⋯的機會

## III. Guided Translation

1. listen; to
2. go; around
3. no; less; than
4. is; sure; to
5. go; in; for

# Round 5
## I. Multiple Choice

| | | | | |
|---|---|---|---|---|
| 1. A | 2. C | 3. D | 4. B | 5. D |
| 6. C | 7. D | 8. A | 9. C | 10. C |
| 11. B | 12. D | 13. B | 14. A | 15. A |
| 16. C | 17. B | 18. A | 19. D | 20. D |

1. 我認為這個產品最符合我的要求。因此，我會買它。
   (A) 要求；(B) 紀念碑；(C) 協議；(D) 文件

2. 城堡被樹木環繞。我們從窗戶看到的一切都是綠色的。
   (A) 威脅；(B) 包，裹；(C) 圍繞；(D) 使驚訝

3. 病患目前正在接受新的肺癌治療。
   (A) 攻擊；(B) 圖表；(C) 四輪馬車；(D) 治療

4. Spencer 女士下週將講授關於企業管理的講座。
   (A) 萵苣；(B) 講座；(C) 手勢；(D) 小畫像

5. 這名企業家認識很多在生意上打過交道的人，但很少有真正的朋友。
   (A) 犯人；(B) 部長；(C) 移民；(D) 泛泛之交

6. 這名政客對網路上散佈謠言的酸民提起訴訟。
   (A) 演講；(B) 束縛；(C) 訴訟；(D) 判決

7. Chris 在買床和書架之前測量了他的臥室。
   (A) 加長；(B) 使混合；(C) 研究；(D) 測量

8. 那間法式餐廳提供的美食和浪漫的氛圍非常受情侶歡迎。
   (A) 氣氛；(B) 專長；(C) 四方型；(D) 推薦

9. 難民急需物資。他們缺衣少食。
   (A) 主管；(B) 表面；(C) 物資；(D) 迷信

10. 種種跡象表明，這名癌症病患很快就會康復。
    (A) 獨立；(B) 個體；(C) 表明；(D) 幻想

11. 在這場國際會議上，你可以遇到不同國籍的人。
    (A) 進退兩難；(B) 國籍；(C) 當局；(D) 人類

12. Olivia 是我最好的朋友。我經常和她分享我的悲傷和快樂。
    (A) 枕頭；(B) 坑洞；(C) 流動；(D) 悲傷

13. 我認為你不能證明僱用童工是正當的。那是不合法的！
    (A) 去除；(B) 僱用；(C) 入侵；(D) 解僱

14. 你有權堅持己見，但同時，你應該聽聽相反的觀點。
    (A) 相反的；(B) 古典的；(C) 棘手的；(D) 過度的

15. 對於某些人來說，休閒服裝意味著 T 恤和牛仔褲。
    (A) 休閒的；(B) 酸的；(C) 健康的；(D) 心靈的

16. Leo 的室友就是如此沒禮貌的傢伙。Leo 怎能容忍他的無禮？
    (A) 表達；(B) 顯示；(C) 容忍；(D) 交換

17. 飛機突然起火燃燒，所有乘客當場死亡。
    (A) 馬車；(B) 火焰；(C) 眼淚；(D) 閃電

18. 不管 Julie 怎麼努力，她仍無法說服老闆接受這個提案。
    (A) 說服；(B) 命令；(C) 退款；(D) 構成

19. 這些規則有點太複雜以至於難以遵循。難怪很多人對它們感到困惑。
    (A) 簡單的；(B) 不情願的；(C) 數位的；(D) 複雜的

20. 那狡詐的員工為了升遷，千方百計討好主管。

(A) 尊重；(B) 鋪 (地面)；(C) 辭職；(D) **討好**

## II. Fill in the Blank

| | | |
|---|---|---|
| 1. shook | 2. wondering | 3. knocked |
| 4. live | 5. care | |

1. 會議開始前，主席向在場的每一位與會者致意並握手。★ shake hands 握手

2. 許多人想知道新任執行長是否有能力改變當地事業。★ wonder 想知道

3. 這名行人頭部中彈，陷入昏迷。
   ★ knock out 使某人無意識或睡著

4. 球員們將竭盡所能達到教練設定的標準。
   ★ live up to sth 達到…

5. Helena 去英國出差前請她哥哥照顧她的寵物貓。★ take care of sb/sth 照顧…

## III. Guided Translation

1. let; down
2. brought; in
3. put; off
4. ran; out; of
5. go; into

# Round 6

## I. Multiple Choice

| 1. D | 2. D | 3. A | 4. D | 5. B |
|---|---|---|---|---|
| 6. A | 7. A | 8. A | 9. C | 10. C |
| 11. A | 12. B | 13. B | 14. D | 15. C |
| 16. B | 17. D | 18. C | 19. C | 20. B |

1. 當我同事 Betty 稱我為工作狂時，我當成一種讚美。
   (A) 賠償金；(B) (音樂) 創作；(C) 成分；(D) **讚美**

2. 那名失蹤的男孩今天下午被發現獨自在街上遊蕩。
   (A) 想知道；(B) 蜿蜒；(C) 破壞；(D) **遊蕩**

3. 這個壞消息讓我倍感震驚。我完全不敢相信。
   (A) **震驚**；(B) 抵抗；(C) 演示；(D) 完成

4. 在冬天，湖面結冰，人們可以在上面滑冰玩樂。
   (A) 尋找；(B) 使害怕；(C) 濫用；(D) **結冰**

5. 遺囑是一種關於某人死後應如何處理其財產或金錢的法律文件。
   (A) 溫和的；(B) **法律上的**；(C) 殖民的；(D) 有霧的

6. 這位歌手在 15 歲時染上了吸菸習慣，現在正在盡最大的努力戒菸。
   (A) **學會**；(B) 需要；(C) 搔癢；(D) 隨信附上

7. 在中國被譽為「詩仙」的李白，是一位名副其實的詩人。
   (A) **值得的**；(B) 嫉妒的；(C) 喜愛的；(D) 體貼的

8. 電動車的日益普及有望減少汽車廢氣排放。
   (A) **排放**；(B) 兌換券；(C) 綜合症；(D) 掠食者

9. Jessica 很難記住她的個人識別碼，所以她下載了一個筆記應用程式來提醒自己。
   (A) 吼叫；(B) 經營；(C) **熟記**；(D) 滑倒

10. 這名求職者被要求將他的照片貼在申請表上。
    (A) 指控；(B) 蒐集；(C) **貼上**；(D) 抓牢

11. 許多動物會儲藏食物並進入深度睡眠以度過冬天。
    (A) **儲藏**；(B) 煽動；(C) 撞，擊；(D) 奮鬥

12. Jack 的生存本能告訴他躺著不要動，假裝死了。
    (A) 閣樓；(B) **本能**；(C) 收益；(D) 密度

13. Nancy 的法語說得很流利，聽起來就像母語人士。
    (A) 國家的；(B) **土生土長的**；(C) 地方性的；(D) 怪異的

14. 你的右眼有東西——試著眨幾次眼睛。
    (A) 覆蓋；(B) 修理 (鞋跟)；(C) 伸長脖子；(D) **眨眼**

15. 在西方文化中，黑貓和數字十三都被認為是厄運的象徵。
    (A) 攀登；(B) (藥物) 一劑；(C) **象徵**；(D) 議題

16. 每個人都必須做點什麼來防止瀕危物種滅絕。
    (A) 獨有的；(B) **瀕臨絕種的**；(C) 優雅的；(D) 巨大的

17. 這些從日本進口的葡萄具有不同於一般葡萄的特殊香氣和滋味。
    (A) 獨特的；(B) 有天分的；(C) 理想的；(D) **一般的**

18. 罷工期間，管理層表示希望與員工直接進行對話。
    (A) 入口；(B) 目錄；(C) **對話**；(D) 合作

19. 這位候選人的競選口號是 「把你的未來交給

我」。

(A) 橡皮擦；(B) 主題；(**C**) **口號**；(D) (報紙的) 標題

20. Jennie 斷然拒絕了我，這讓我很氣餒。

(A) 微弱的；(**B**) **斷然的**；(C) 假的；(D) 健康的

## II. Fill in the Blank

| | | |
|---|---|---|
| 1. shame | 2. left | 3. catch |
| 4. shape | 5. divorced | |

1. 這名政客在電視節目中發表的惡意言論讓他的政黨蒙羞。★ shame 恥辱

2. 這名丈夫拋下妻子，再也沒有回到她身邊。
   ★ leave sb/sth behind 拋下…

3. 印花洋裝會再次成為最時尚的服裝嗎？
   ★ catch on 變得流行；變得受歡迎

4. 為了吸引小孩注意，麵包師把餅乾做成動物形狀。★ in the shape of 呈…的形狀

5. 大多數球迷只是希望看到最優秀的運動員為熱愛運動而競爭，且認為體育應該脫離政治。
   ★ divorce 脫離

## III. Guided Translation

1. do; away; with
2. lies; in
3. by; air
4. tell; from
5. keep; promise

# Round 7

## I. Multiple Choice

| | | | | |
|---|---|---|---|---|
| 1. B | 2. A | 3. C | 4. A | 5. C |
| 6. B | 7. D | 8. D | 9. A | 10. D |
| 11. B | 12. B | 13. A | 14. D | 15. C |
| 16. D | 17. B | 18. C | 19. C | 20. A |

1. Timothy 非常害羞，在全班同學面前發表演講時臉都紅了。
   (A) 使集中；(**B**) **臉紅**；(C) (使) 滑動；(D) 困住

2. Daphne 是能隨機應變的人。她能輕易適應新環境。
   (**A**) **可變通的**；(B) 有說服力的；(C) 優雅的；(D)

熱帶的

3. 魔術師向兔子揮了揮魔杖，讓牠消失。
   (A) 拜訪；(B) 重視；(**C**) **消失**；(D) 認為

4. 這間醫院創立於 1920 年。從那時起一直服務病患。
   (**A**) **創立**；(B) 摺疊；(C) 燃燒；(D) 搧 (風)

5. 由於需求量大，批發商無法保證外用酒精和口罩的供應量足夠。
   (A) (疾病) 接觸性傳染的；(B) 有效的；(**C**) **足夠的**；(D) 可替代的

6. 兩國之間的邊界爭端造成了緊張局勢。
   (A) 重要；(**B**) **情況**；(C) 簽名；(D) 真誠

7. 總統在演講中特別提到這名士兵，讓他感到非常榮幸。
   (A) 努力；(B) 關係；(C) 用途；(**D**) **提及**

8. 政治難民試圖與外界聯繫都沒有成功。
   (A) 警告；(B) 審判；(C) 療法；(**D**) **嘗試**

9. 公車或捷運是我母親上班的交通工具。
   (**A**) **交通工具**；(B) 讚賞；(C) 消化；(D) 專注

10. Gina 今早上班遲到，因為她塞車塞了一個小時。
    (A) 寶石；(B) 果凍；(C) 下巴；(**D**) **堵塞**

11. 經理太固執了。他不可能改變主意。
    (A) 光榮的；(**B**) **固執的**；(C) 勤勉的；(D) 精力充沛的

12. 我們都希望長久的世界和平，沒有國家會與另一國起衝突。
    (A) 實際的；(**B**) **持久的**；(C) 內部的；(D) 家庭的

13. 如果說蘋果是有機種植的，那就代表農夫沒有使用化學肥料。
    (**A**) **有機地**；(B) 生物學地；(C) 節約地；(D) 有效地

14. 為了拯救海洋生物，人們必須停止倒垃圾至海洋。
    (A) 許可；(B) 保護；(C) 練習；(**D**) **停止**

15. 在電力驅動的車輛發明之前，人們主要使用汽油作為動力。
    (A) 實現；(B) 繁榮；(**C**) **汽油**；(D) 康復

16. 醫生給 Williams 先生做檢查，並告訴他一切正常。
    (A) 攝影師；(B) 哲學家；(C) 物理學家；(**D**) (**尤指內科**) **醫師**

17. 地球村的概念現已廣泛被大眾接受。
    (A) 擔心；(**B**) **概念**；(C) 平等；(D) 分析

18. 那名飛行員在飛機失事後奇蹟般的生還已成為一個傳奇。即使在十年後，它仍然被記得和談論。
    (A) (入室) 竊賊；(B) 花生；(**C**) **傳說**；(D) 插座

19. 父親抱著孩子，輕聲哼著搖籃曲給她聽。
    (A) 擁抱；(B) 敲擊；(**C**) **哼歌**；(D) 使安靜

20. 長假期間，風景區被大量遊客湧入。
    (**A**) **湧入**；(B) 禱告；(C) 恢復；(D) 調查

## II. Fill in the Blank

| | | |
|---|---|---|
| 1. afford | 2. panic | 3. shelter |
| 4. question | 5. transferred | |

1. 這家人連生活用品都無法負擔，更別說買房了。★ afford 負擔得起

2. 儘管健行者在森林中迷路，但他並沒有驚慌失措，並設法找到了一條出路。
   ★ get into a panic 慌張起來

3. 由於傾盆大雨，路人紛紛躲避至門口。
   ★ take shelter 躲避

4. Watson 一家幾乎無法維持生計，度假對他們而言是不可能的。
   ★ be out of the question 不可能

5. Emily 與其他三名工程師一起從總部被調到巴黎分公司。★ transfer (使) 調動

## III. Guided Translation

| |
|---|
| 1. look; out |
| 2. Put; down |
| 3. valid; for |
| 4. in; case |
| 5. ups; downs |

# Round 8

## I. Multiple Choice

| 1. C | 2. D | 3. B | 4. A | 5. A |
|---|---|---|---|---|
| 6. C | 7. C | 8. B | 9. B | 10. D |
| 11. D | 12. A | 13. A | 14. D | 15. C |
| 16. B | 17. C | 18. A | 19. C | 20. B |

1. 水電工逆時針轉動螺絲，將其鬆開。
   (A) 辛勞工作；(B) 加長；(**C**) **鬆開**；(D) 淹水

2. 經濟蕭條導致許多小企業破產。
   (A) 穩定；(B) 附件；(C) 盲目；(**D**) **破產**

3. 運動有很多好處。例如，它可以幫助你增強體力。
   (A) 溼度；(**B**) **力氣**；(C) 信仰；(D) 爆炸

4. 在中華文化，穿著紅色或其他鮮豔的顏色參加葬禮是非常不合適的。
   (**A**) **葬禮**；(B) 發射；(C) 教堂；(D) 婚禮

5. 勞累了一天之後，沿著海灘悠閒散步很放鬆。
   (**A**) **悠閒的**；(B) 致命的；(C) 傻的；(D) 貴的

6. 這些年來，該政黨已傾向採取更溫和的政策。
   (A) 使適應；(B) 調整；(**C**) **採取**；(D) 建議

7. 在輪班 12 小時後，護理師感到睏倦並打哈欠。
   (A) 睡著的；(B) 醒著的；(**C**) **睏倦的**；(D) 糟糕的

8. 我認為每個家庭成員都應該幫助做家務。
   (A) 心理的；(**B**) **家庭的**；(C) 最後的；(D) 直接的

9. 被槍指著的戰俘向他的敵人求饒。
   (A) 接受；(**B**) **仁慈**；(C) 幫助；(D) 女用襯衫

10. 擁有正向的生活態度，Bill 能以健康的方式應對緊張的局面。
    (A) 嫉妒；(B) 中斷；(C) 偏好；(**D**) **態度**

11. Paula 聳了肩說她不知道這個計畫。
    (A) 拳頭；(B) 手掌；(C) 脖子；(**D**) **肩膀**

12. 智慧型手機不再是豪華的現代設備。它已成為許多人的必需品。
    (**A**) **必需品**；(B) 龍蝦；(C) 大批；(D) 取向

13. 有些父母以誇耀孩子的非凡成就為樂。
    (**A**) **誇耀**；(B) 取笑；(C) 抱怨；(D) 遵從

14. Matilda 很珍惜她深愛的祖母死後留給她的珍珠項鍊。
    (A) 確定；(B) 管理；(C) 浪費；(**D**) **珍惜**

15. 如果課堂紀律執行不當，就會出現混亂。
    (A) 咯咯笑；(B) 負擔得起；**(C) 執行**；(D) 繼續做

16. 聯合國是個旨在促進國際合作與世界和平的組織。
    (A) 住宿；**(B) 組織**；(C) 特殊場合；(D) 請願書

17. 這款折疊智慧型手機折疊後只有 8 公分長。
    (A) 公尺；(B) 公里；**(C) 公分**；(D) 英尺

18. 所有的田徑運動項目都會很有競爭力和挑戰性。
    **(A) 小徑**；(B) 距離；(C) 選擇；(D) 重量

19. 許多人沒有意識到未經許可在網路下載影片或音樂會構成剽竊。
    (A) 加工處理；(B) 蒐集；**(C) 剽竊**；(D) 正式告知

20. 我想確認我八月十二日的單人房預訂。
    (A) 承認；**(B) 確認**；(C) 做出結論；(D) 通勤

## II. Fill in the Blank

| | | |
|---|---|---|
| 1. picture | 2. center | 3. shine |
| 4. effort | 5. amounted | |

1. 無論目擊者如何努力解釋，警方仍無法了解事情的全貌。★ get the picture 了解情況

2. 把花瓶放在桌子中央，這樣它就不會被撞倒。
   ★ in the center of sth 在…的中心

3. 風雨無阻，郵遞員每天都會定時投遞郵件。
   ★ rain or shine 風雨無阻；無論如何

4. Miley 不遺餘力地幫助無家可歸的小孩。
   ★ spare no effort 不遺餘力

5. 據新聞報導，水災遇難人數已達二十人。
   ★ amount to sth 達到；總計

## III. Guided Translation

1. turn; down
2. held; up
3. mixed; up
4. or; so
5. Hold; on

# Round 9

## I. Multiple Choice

| | | | | |
|---|---|---|---|---|
| 1. C | 2. C | 3. A | 4. B | 5. D |
| 6. B | 7. B | 8. B | 9. C | 10. D |
| 11. D | 12. D | 13. C | 14. A | 15. B |
| 16. D | 17. A | 18. A | 19. C | 20. A |

1. 優惠券和折扣創造誘因讓購物者在超市購買更多商品。
   (A) 強度；(B) 互動；**(C) 誘因**；(D) 自主性

2. 市民的投訴多到不容忽視，政府必須採取行動解決問題。
   (A) 年資較淺的；(B) 寬敞的；**(C) 大量的**；(D) 好奇的

3. 明年將在該地點建造一座新的摩天大樓。
   **(A) 地點**；(B) 觀點；(C) 成長；(D) 電梯

4. 那輛車正在逐漸加快速度。它變得越來越快。
   (A) 減少；**(B) 漸增**；(C) 準備；(D) 抵達

5. 一個開明的社會應該是寬容的，允許不同的思想和信仰存在。
   (A) 行政的；(B) 激進的；(C) 傳統的；**(D) 開明的**

6. 在面試前，在網路尋找一些關於該公司的資訊對你來說是有利的。
   (A) 有冒險精神的；**(B) 有利的**；(C) 迅速的；(D) 豐富的

7. 這座木橋太脆弱以至於無法支撐那輛沉重的卡車。
   (A) 投降；**(B) 支撐**；(C) 關住；(D) 拉，拖

8. 這位心理學家目前在研究人類行為。
   (A) 空心的；**(B) 人類的**；(C) 每小時的；(D) 水平的

9. 和父母住在一起的好處之一就是不用付房租。
   (A) 劣勢；(B) 物質；**(C) 優點**；(D) 性格

10. 這位著名的科學家向全世界的觀眾發表了演講。
    (A) 麥克筆；(B) 兄弟姊妹；(C) 學期；**(D) 觀眾**

11. 送貨員被大雨淋得渾身濕透。
    (A) 懈怠的；(B) 模糊的；(C) 被動的；**(D) 溼透的**

12. 大多數人認為那名罪犯遲早會被繩之以法。
    (A) 偏見；(B) 廢棄物；(C) 損傷；**(D) 正義**

13. 員工們很失望，老闆對他們提出的加薪要求給

了一個否定的答案。
(A) 普遍的；(B) 數不清的；(C) **負面的**；(D) 嚴重的

14. 英文從法文和德文中借用了許多詞。
(A) **借用**；(B) 借出；(C) 找到；(D) 發明

15. 那名獵人用步槍向鹿射擊，但沒打中。
(A) 剃去 (毛髮)；(B) **射擊**；(C) 移動；(D) 搖動

16. Tommy 看到他的弟弟得到一輛新腳踏車作為生日禮物，感到一陣羨慕。
(A) 傾向；(B) 妄想；(C) 財產；(D) **羨慕**

17. 這名律師是一個有條理的人。甚至她的書都是按字母順序排列的。
(A) **有條理的**；(B) 有教養的；(C) 行為端正的；
(D) 見多識廣的

18. 我不認為我可以繼續做這份工作。這對我來說太有難度了。
(A) **有難度的**；(B) 自動的；(C) 適當的；(D) 寬鬆的

19. Maggie 把維他命片切成兩半，因為它太大了以至於她無法吞嚥。
(A) 吐出；(B) 用螺絲固定；(C) **吞嚥**；(D) 發誓

20. 總統選舉後，政黨內部隨後發生了數月的衝突。
(A) **跟隨而來**；(B) 資助；(C) 過濾；(D) 固定

## II. Fill in the Blank

| | | |
|---|---|---|
| 1. certain | 2. acquaintance | 3. furious |
| 4. supposed | 5. chance | |

1. 即使雙方都同意停火，又如何確保雙方都不會再打破協議呢？★ make certain 確保

2. 我對作者了解不多。我對他的書只略知一二。
★ have a nodding acquaintance with sb/sth 對…略知一二

3. Kevin 的父母對他很生氣，因為他昨晚很晚才回家。★ furious 極其生氣的

4. 由於即將來臨的颱風可能會造成損失，我們應該提前做些準備。★ be supposed to 應該

5. Doris 意外得到這份工作。她碰巧是唯一的求職者。★ by chance 意外地

## III. Guided Translation

1. lived; on
2. in; shoes
3. make; peace
4. took; turns
5. hold; back

# Round 10

## I. Multiple Choice

| | | | | |
|---|---|---|---|---|
| 1. B | 2. C | 3. A | 4. C | 5. B |
| 6. D | 7. C | 8. D | 9. D | 10. A |
| 11. C | 12. D | 13. B | 14. A | 15. A |
| 16. A | 17. B | 18. B | 19. C | 20. D |

1. 我不想錯過一年一度的音樂節。畢竟，它一年只舉辦一次。
(A) 私人的；(B) **一年一度的**；(C) 道德的；(D) 微妙的

2. Pete 只能透過手電筒微弱的光線看到前面的路。
(A) 豆 (英)；(B) 珠子；(C) **光線**；(D) 戰鬥

3. 一個未經訓練的健行者爬上這麼陡峭的懸崖絕非易事。
(A) **陡峭的**；(B) 穩定的；(C) 穩定的；(D) 規範的

4. 遊客們抬起頭，驚奇地凝望著明亮的星星。
(A) 瞥見；(B) 怒視；(C) **凝視**；(D) 抓住

5. 有些民主國家的人可能不理解自由的真正含義並容易濫用自由。
(A) 教育；(B) **自由**；(C) 喜愛；(D) 能力

6. 客隊的表現受到炎熱天氣的影響，因此輸掉了比賽。
(A) 減少；(B) 傷害；(C) 熱愛；(D) **影響**

7. 頭痛、喉嚨痛、疲勞和肌肉酸痛都是流感的典型症狀。
(A) 次要的；(B) 赤裸的；(C) **典型的**；(D) 怪異的

8. 因為戰爭，通貨膨脹率達到了前所未有的程度。
(A) 認知的；(B) 可持續的；(C) 富有想像力的；
(D) **史無前例的**

9. Bob 目前沒空。我要請他回電給你嗎？
(A) 能夠負擔的；(B) 連續的；(C) 集體的；(D) **有空的**

10. Jessica 在轉行娛樂業之前曾從事 YouTuber。
(A) **轉移**；(B) 清掃；(C) 縫補；(D) 猜想

11. 小男孩從腳踏車上摔下來，褲子膝蓋處破了。
(A) 手肘；(B) 手臂；(C) **膝蓋**；(D) 大拇指

12. 那對父母遭控疏於照顧他們的孩子，因為他們未能提供孩子們適當的食物和照顧。
(A) 主宰；(B) 容忍；(C) 毀掉；(D) **疏於照顧**

13. 在週末經常可以看到購物者在跳蚤市場與攤販討價還價。
(A) 接線生；(B) **攤販**；(C) 叛徒；(D) 驚悚片

14. 這消息來源可靠。它應該是準確的。
(A) **來源**；(B) 節奏；(C) 研究機構；(D) (詩、歌) 節

15. 技術人員的工作是評估新材料如何耐得住磨損。
(A) **評估**；(B) 回收利用；(C) 承諾；(D) 構成

16. 河岸邊那間時髦的餐廳原先是間船庫。
(A) **原先地**；(B) 反常地；(C) 有害地；(D) 密集的

17. 結冰的路面很滑以至於我們幾乎站不好。
(A) 堅固的；(B) **溼滑的**；(C) 不新鮮的；(D) 鹹的

18. 因為意識形態的衝突，墮胎在許多國家是個有爭議的話題。
(A) 草茂密的；(B) **引起爭議的**；(C) 橢圓形的；(D) 不可思議的

19. 火車三點整從 4 號月臺出發。
(A) 舞臺；(B) 厚紙板；(C) **月臺**；(D) 儀表板

20. 這場大火對這座具有歷史意義的建築物造成了相當大的破壞。
(A) 有建設性的；(B) 不停的；(C) 不斷的；(D) **相當大的**

## II. Fill in the Blank

| | | |
|---|---|---|
| 1. mistake | 2. appreciation | 3. burst |
| 4. compromise | 5. doubt | |

1. 這位外國遊客不小心搭上錯的公車，讓他離目的地更遠了。★ by mistake 錯誤地

2. 一位政治難民拍影片感謝聯合國的援助。
★ in appreciation of 感謝…

3. Amy 迷路又不知所措，在火車站突然哭起來。
★ burst into tears 突然哭起來

4. 經過長時間的談話，Allen 和他的妻子終於對

家事議題達成協議。
★ reach a compromise 達成妥協

5. 威廉·莎士比亞創作了許多偉大的戲劇和詩歌，無疑是最有影響力的英語作家之一。
★ beyond doubt 無庸置疑

## III. Guided Translation

1. baby; shower
2. dried; up
3. help; to
4. chat; with
5. at; first; sight

# Round 11

## I. Multiple Choice

| | | | | |
|---|---|---|---|---|
| 1. B | 2. D | 3. B | 4. C | 5. C |
| 6. B | 7. D | 8. C | 9. A | 10. C |
| 11. C | 12. A | 13. A | 14. D | 15. D |
| 16. D | 17. B | 18. A | 19. B | 20. A |

1. 以機器人取代工人的原因是為了降低生產成本。
(A) 驅散；(B) **取代**；(C) 冒犯；(D) 移動

2. 父親輕輕推動搖籃，讓他哭鬧的嬰兒平靜下來。
(A) 裂縫；(B) 起重機；(C) 蠟筆；(D) **搖籃**

3. 傳記說，莫札特在三歲時就表現出非凡的音樂天賦。
(A) 永恆的；(B) **優異的**；(C) 可疑的；(D) 有害的

4. 環保人士反對核能發電。
(A) 悲慘；(B) 成熟；(C) **產生，發生**；(D) 短缺

5. 一道閃電擊中機艙並引發火災。
(A) 刀片；(B) 化學；(C) **閃電**；(D) 斜坡

6. 這隻狗極具攻擊性。牠對每一個路人狂吠。
(A) 大面積的；(B) **有攻擊性的**；(C) 令人愉快的；(D) 值得讚賞的

7. 這家電子公司有 485 名正職員工。
(A) 東西；(B) 爐灶；(C) 吸管；(D) **員工**

8. 有些鸚鵡能夠模仿人類的語言。
(A) 口譯；(B) 分配；(C) **模仿**；(D) 融合

9. 醫生正在顯微鏡下檢查血球。
   (A) **顯微鏡**；(B) 微波爐；(C) 電報；(D) 望遠鏡

10. 這位宗教領袖因對世界和平有重大貢獻而被授予諾貝爾和平獎。
    (A) 競爭；(B) 維持；(C) **授予**；(D) 醒來

11. 老師在教室後面的黑板上貼了一張關於班規的告示。
    (A) 漂流；(B) 緩慢行進；(C) **黏貼**；(D) 螫，叮

12. 分公司經理必須與員工們協商，以便盡早結束罷工。
    (A) **協商**；(B) 溜冰；(C) 結合；(D) 打鬥

13. 網球員不停地拍球讓它彈到牆上。
    (A) **彈起**；(B) 撞上；(C) 碰傷；(D) 保佑

14. 記得在寄出信封之前貼上一張郵票。
    (A) 水龍頭；(B) 繩結；(C) 港口；(D) **郵票**

15. 粗略估算，我會在下週二之前完成工作。
    (A) 商人；(B) 診斷；(C) (房屋) 貸款或抵押；(D) **估算**

16. 駕駛側有一道刮痕，但除此之外，汽車狀況良好。
    (A) 然而；(B) 所以；(C) 而且；(D) **除此之外**

17. Belinda 是我國第一位奧運會網球冠軍。
    (A) 省；(B) **冠軍**；(C) 錦標賽；(D) 評審團

18. Rachel 對花粉過敏，每次去祖母的花園時都會吸鼻子。
    (A) **吸鼻子**；(B) 戲弄；(C) 低語；(D) 當家庭教師

19. 員工會議上，老闆宣布因為經濟不景氣，不發年終獎金。
    (A) 打斷；(B) **宣布**；(C) 爆炸；(D) 原諒

20. 脫口秀主持人的幽默感為他在全國贏得了很高的人氣。
    (A) **受歡迎**；(B) 人口；(C) 汙染；(D) (音樂) 創作

## II. Fill in the Blank

| 1. moment | 2. butterflies | 3. similar |
|---|---|---|
| 4. kind | 5. matter | |

1. 由於沒有人來認領遭竊的汽車，警方只能暫時保管。★ for the moment 暫時

2. Oscar 在搭雲霄飛車前感到異常緊張。
   ★ have butterflies (in your stomach) 感到非常緊張

3. 地球的形狀和橘子相似。★ similar 相似的

4. Ivan 邀請暗戀對象參加他的生日派對時有點緊張。★ kind of (用於表示不確定) 有點

5. 無論前方有什麼阻礙，我們都不會放棄。
   ★ no matter what 無論什麼

## III. Guided Translation

1. make; both; ends; meet
2. take; apart
3. threw; away
4. of; any; help
5. arm; in; arm

# Round 12

## I. Multiple Choice

| 1. A | 2. D | 3. D | 4. B | 5. C |
|---|---|---|---|---|
| 6. A | 7. D | 8. C | 9. A | 10. B |
| 11. A | 12. C | 13. B | 14. C | 15. B |
| 16. D | 17. D | 18. A | 19. B | 20. C |

1. 我們決定延後會議直到經理休假回來。
   (A) **延後**；(B) 鑲了框；(C) 刪除；(D) 犧牲

2. 隨著現代科技的快速發展，50 年後的生活會是什麼樣子真的很難預測。
   (A) 較喜歡；(B) 呈現；(C) 假裝；(D) **預測**

3. 根據事故目擊者所稱，那輛超速行駛的汽車撞上了火車。
   (A) 製造商；(B) 平民；(C) 科學家；(D) **目擊者**

4. 隨著全球暖化的影響越來越嚴重，每個人都應該努力減少自己的碳足跡。
   (A) 電動的；(B) **全球的**；(C) 熱的，溫的；(D) 有權力的

5. 做這道菜的第一步是煮蔬菜，直到所有的液體都被蔬菜吸收。
   (A) 量；(B) 固體；(C) **液體**；(D) 地基

6. 根據報導，該演員與一名已婚婦女有段風流韻事。
   (A) **風流韻事**；(B) 文明；(C) 手工藝；(D) 想像力

7. 湖的北邊部分很淺。船可能觸底。

(A) 巨大的；(B) 易接近的；(C) 直言不諱的；(D) **淺的**

8. 你對法律的無知總有一天會給你帶來麻煩。
   (A) 參與；(B) 無罪；(C) **無知**；(D) 改進

9. 我討厭成為第一個抵達聚會的人 —— 這讓我感到尷尬。
   (A) **尷尬的**；(B) 血腥的；(C) 溫馴的；(D) 原子的

10. 看到門口有空位，那名乘客趕緊跑去坐下。
    (A) 肥沃的；(B) **空的**；(C) 異常的；(D) 匆忙的

11. 這位政治領導人聲稱在該國執行嚴格的紀律是合理的。
    (A) **紀律**；(B) 結果；(C) 菜餚；(D) 武器

12. Sylvia 住在一個有很多扒手和毒販的危險住宅區。
    (A) 預防措施；(B) 工作；(C) **住宅區**；(D) 地形

13. 聚會結束後，Wendy 決定搭計程車回家。雖然這主人願意載她一程，她不想給他添額外的麻煩。
    (A) 買賣；(B) **麻煩**；(C) 驚恐；(D) 需要

14. Frank 認為孩子是父母離婚的可憐受害者。
    (A) 會計師；(B) 評論家；(C) **受害者**；(D) 申請者

15. 除了飛機誤點一個小時外，這是一趟完美的旅程。
    (A) 名聲；(B) **例外**；(C) 期望；(D) 歡迎會

16. 在計算最後一張選票之前，選舉的結果是不確定的。
    (A) 大綱；(B) 零售店；(C) 服裝；(D) **結果**

17. 被控兩項謀殺罪的男子已被判處二十年徒刑。
    (A) 討價還價；(B) 違抗；(C) 要求；(D) **控告**

18. 違反交通規則的駕駛應該為他們的不當行為受處罰。
    (A) **違反**；(B) 誤導；(C) 遵守；(D) 批准

19. Aaron 向 Joan 尋求建議，因為她是室內設計的資訊來源。
    (A) 信徒；(B) **泉源**；(C) 財富；(D) 組成

20. 世界上仍有一定比例的人口缺乏足夠的營養。
    (A) 種類；(B) (生物分類) 種；(C) **人口**；(D) 協定

## II. Fill in the Blank

| 1. while | 2. seated | 3. earnest |
|---|---|---|
| 4. mention | 5. arrest | |

1. 如果你偶爾才運動，我不認為你有辦法減重。
   ★ (every) once in a while 偶爾；有時

2. 客人全部入座後，我們開始用餐。
   ★ seat yourself 使坐下

3. 通知寫道六月一日正式開始在職培訓。
   ★ in earnest 正式地；完全地

4. Christine 是我面試過的最有創新精神、最聰明，更不用說才華橫溢的求職者之一。
   ★ not to mention 更不用說

5. 那名搶匪在銀行外被攔住後被捕。
   ★ put sb under arrest 逮捕某人

## III. Guided Translation

1. woke; up
2. make; yourself; at; home
3. had; no; choice; but; to
4. all; walks; of; life
5. gotten; hooked; on

# Round 13

## I. Multiple Choice

| 1. D | 2. D | 3. C | 4. B | 5. D |
|---|---|---|---|---|
| 6. C | 7. A | 8. B | 9. C | 10. A |
| 11. D | 12. B | 13. D | 14. C | 15. D |
| 16. A | 17. A | 18. A | 19. C | 20. B |

1. 現今人們使用相機應用程式或照片編輯器來隱藏皮膚瑕疵是很常見的。
   (A) 結冰；(B) 分割；(C) 抗議；(D) **隱藏**

2. 外面正在下雨。我們今天晚餐何不點外送披薩呢？
   (A) 決定；(B) 使沮喪；(C) 揭露；(D) **運送**

3. 你知道達陣一次得多少分嗎？
   (A) 偵查；(B) 責罵；(C) **得分**；(D) 刷洗

4. 鵝媽媽創作的童謠在一些國家屬於公共財。
   (A) (政黨等經選舉獲得的) 授權；(B) **領域，範圍**；(C) 神學；(D) 獨立存在的個體，實體

5. 在美國許多州，販酒給 21 歲以下的人是違法的。
   (A) 金屬；(B) 電力；(C) 鮪魚；**(D) 含酒精飲料**

6. 三架敵機在邊界被擊落。
   (A) 船；(B) 乘船遊覽；**(C) 飛機**；(D) 火車

7. 即使時局艱難，這位職業運動員仍然努力練習，永不放棄。
   **(A) 艱難的**；(B) 都市的；(C) 厚的；(D) 單獨的

8. 越來越多人希望移民到一個政治紛爭更少的國家。
   (A) 包含；**(B) 移民**；(C) 偽造；(D) 出現

9. 我出國旅行時會盡量少帶行李。我喜歡輕裝旅行。
   (A) 小麥；(B) 喜好；**(C) 行李**；(D) 失業 (率)

10. 我第一次去東京的時候，對那裡複雜的鐵路網感到困惑。
    **(A) 網狀系統**；(B) 架構；(C) 煙火；(D) 家事

11. 我們要學會看事物的光明面以及要有積極的生活態度。
    (A) 薄片；(B) 脊椎；(C) 床單；**(D) 面**

12. 戰區人民急需食品和醫療救助。物資幾乎耗盡了。
    (A) 排除；**(B) 耗盡**；(C) 促進；(D) 維持

13. 處理工作時，Bob 往往過於樂觀而忽略了未來可能遇到的困難。
    (A) 超過；(B) 推翻；(C) 翻倒；**(D) 忽略**

14. 一群婦女發起了反對工作場所性別歧視的運動。
    (A) 聚集；(B) 暴動；**(C) 發起**；(D) 引述

15. 體育場是一個四周都有座位的大型運動場。
    (A) 攝影棚，錄音室；(B) 條，帶，細長條；(C) 雕像；**(D) 體育場**

16. 同事散布關於 Anna 的辦公室八卦，這讓她感到震怒。
    **(A) 狂怒的**；(B) 強制性的；(C) 武裝的；(D) 財政稅收的，金融的

17. Mila 野外露營時，總會帶個可攜式瓦斯爐。
    **(A) 可攜的**；(B) 顯著的；(C) 多變的；(D) 暗的

18. 兩國邊界的爭端應在歷史背景充足下被理解。
    **(A) (事情發生的) 背景**；(B) 大陸，大洲；(C) 比賽；(D) 技師

19. 我擦這個牌了的香水是因為我喜歡它的木質香。
    (A) 僧侶；(B) 品種；**(C) 品牌**；(D) 新聞記者

20. Willy 夢想著中樂透，成為百萬富翁，從此過上奢華的生活。
    (A) 黃銅；**(B) 百萬富翁**；(C) 乳房；(D) 合約

## II. Fill in the Blank

| | | |
|---|---|---|
| 1. revenge | 2. waved | 3. honor |
| 4. complaining | 5. circumstances | |

1. 故事的最後，這位女子報復了背叛她的丈夫。
   ★ take revenge on sb 向某人復仇

2. Fiona 走出商店後，銷售員在門口向她揮手告別。★ wave goodbye (to sb) 揮手告別某人

3. 我們舉行晚宴向一位即將退休的老師致敬。
   ★ in honor of 向…表敬意

4. Tina 總是抱怨丈夫沒用。★ complain 抱怨

5. 無論如何 Annie 的父親都不會同意她嫁給那名老先生。
   ★ under no circumstances 無論如何不

## III. Guided Translation

1. broke; the; news; to
2. at; ease
3. rather; than
4. Except; for
5. clears; up

# Round 14

## I. Multiple Choice

| 1. B | 2. D | 3. A | 4. D | 5. A |
|---|---|---|---|---|
| 6. D | 7. B | 8. A | 9. C | 10. C |
| 11. B | 12. C | 13. D | 14. B | 15. A |
| 16. B | 17. C | 18. C | 19. A | 20. C |

1. 這個國家的所有工作者都有最低工資的保障，他們的薪資不得低於此。
   (A) 傲慢的；**(B) 最小極限的**；(C) 最多的；(D) 有說服力的

2. 教練喊了暫停，讓運動員休息幾秒鐘喘口氣。

(A) 自殺；(B) 索引；(C) 棲息地；**(D) 呼吸**

3. 這名作者最新的詩集受到了文學評論家的好評。
**(A) 文學的**；(B) 結構上的；(C) 最大極限的；(D) 最少的

4. 火災發生時，那位居民盡可能大聲尖叫引起警覺。
(A) 騙子；(B) 垃圾；(C) 手勢；**(D) 警報**

5. 這名男孩正吃著一碗撒有迷你棉花糖的冰淇淋。
**(A) 撒，灑**；(B) 使失調；(C) 低估；(D) 想知道

6. 出生率下降正影響著該國的人口、教育和經濟。
(A) (將資訊) 輸入；(B) 輕輕地拍；(C) 攻擊；**(D) 影響**

7. Joseph 擅長做麵包和蛋糕，因為他曾在當地一家麵包店工作。
(A) 苗圃；**(B) 麵包店**；(C) 市場；(D) 車站

8. Ellen 買了些磁鐵和鑰匙圈作為羅馬之行的紀念品。
**(A) 紀念品**；(B) 策略；(C) 主題；(D) 解決辦法

9. 以色列在第二次世界大戰後成立國家。
(A) 提及；(B) 參加者；**(C) 存在**；(D) 開花

10. John 非常擅長修理房子周圍的東西，因此被取了「巧手先生」的綽號。
(A) 認出；(B) 貼標籤；**(C) 取綽號**；(D) 描述特點

11. 臺灣的大多數高中生應該都穿校服上學。
(A) 雨傘；**(B) 制服**；(C) 整體性；(D) 工會

12. 未能履行義務的員工被解僱了。
(A) 工廠；(B) 盤問；**(C) 達到 (目標)**；(D) 鑽

13. 該獎項將授予在科學領域做出重大發現的傑出工作者。
(A) 精神的；(B) 明顯的；(C) 潛在的；**(D) 傑出的**

14. 那輛警車開得真快。肯定是在追捕某人。
(A) 縫紉；**(B) 追捕**；(C) 安慰；(D) 使痛苦

15. 用刀切菜時要小心，因為刀片非常鋒利。
**(A) 銳利的**；(B) 光滑的；(C) 生鏽的；(D) 明白清楚的

16. 執行長排除了這個主意，認為不值得考慮。
(A) 搜索；**(B) (從頭腦中) 去除**；(C) 錯過；(D) 犯 (罪、錯)

17. 人們在寄信時必須支付郵資。
(A) 海報；(B) 明信片；**(C) 郵資**；(D) 延期

18. 貓眼的發明為道路安全做出了重大貢獻。
(A) 決定；(B) 分配；**(C) 貢獻**；(D) 交叉 (口)

19. 當房客拒絕為他對公寓造成的損害負責時，房東氣瘋了。
**(A) 責任**；(B) 詢問；(C) 和諧；(D) 死亡數量

20. 我鄰居散布別人流言的方式真的惹惱我了。
(A) 溝通；(B) 遮蔽；**(C) 散布流言**；(D) 拭去灰塵

## II. Fill in the Blank

| | | |
|---|---|---|
| 1. economical | 2. associated | 3. hunting |
| 4. watch | 5. side | |

1. Hill 先生很節省時間和金錢。他從不浪費。
★ economical 節約的；省錢的

2. 在中華文化，紅色往往與好運聯想在一起。
★ be associated with sth 把…聯想在一起

3. 警方已經在樹林裡尋找失蹤的小孩兩天了。
★ hunt for sb/sth 搜尋…

4. 這位億萬富翁僱傭了很多保鑣全天候看守他和他的家人。★ watch over sb 看守；照看

5. 止咳藥對我的心臟有副作用，現在心跳得很快。
★ side effect 副作用

## III. Guided Translation

1. Best; of; all
2. occurred; to
3. under; the; weather
4. down; in; the; dumps
5. get; rid; of

# Round 15

## I. Multiple Choice

| | | | | |
|---|---|---|---|---|
| 1. C | 2. C | 3. A | 4. B | 5. B |
| 6. C | 7. A | 8. B | 9. B | 10. D |
| 11. A | 12. D | 13. C | 14. D | 15. B |
| 16. C | 17. A | 18. D | 19. A | 20. D |

1. 應徵者出色的自我介紹給面試官留下了深刻的印象。

(A) 讚賞；(B) 做記號；(C) **給…留下深刻印象**；
(D) 使沮喪

2. 一直往前走，你可以在你的左手邊看到郵局。
(A) 四處；(B) 粗魯地；(C) **直直地**；(D) 到處

3. 這位著名的外科醫生已經進行了無數次成功的手術。
(A) **外科醫生**；(B) 代理商；(C) 商人；(D) 製作人

4. 那名芭蕾舞者舞姿優美，我們都目不轉睛地看著她。
(A) 可能；(B) **優雅地**；(C) 深切地；(D) 大概

5. 妻小離開後，這個失業的男人開始酗酒，每天都虛度光陰。
(A) 檸檬汁；(B) **酒**；(C) 醋；(D) 蒸氣

6. Brown 女士有無限的耐心，非常適合教導小孩子。
(A) 調查；(B) 繼承；(C) **適合**；(D) 使困惑

7. 少數民族的利益和權利應受到尊重和保護。
(A) **少數族體**；(B) 同儕；(C) 良心；(D) 行為

8. 由於 Howard 快要禿頭了，他看起來比實際年齡老很多。
(A) 小巧的；(B) **禿頭**；(C) 可惡的；(D) 勇敢的

9. 勇敢的救生員毫不畏懼地在湖中救了一個溺水的男孩。
(A) 懇求；(B) **表露**；(C) 延遲；(D) 穿線

10. 小女孩從可怕的惡夢中驚醒，哭個不停。
(A) 擁護者；(B) 視力；(C) 直覺；(D) **惡夢**

11. 司機踩了剎車，但令他驚恐的是車子並沒有減速。
(A) **剎車**；(B) 盤子；(C) 後車箱；(D) 中斷

12. 從芬蘭搬到巴西，Tyler 花了一年適應新環境。
(A) 約會；(B) 立場；(C) 道德；(D) **環境**

13. 社會公平是指一定社會內的所有個體皆享有平等的自由、權利和取得公物的機會。
(A) 程度；(B) 生態系統；(C) **公平**；(D) 專家

14. 別忘了還你欠 Peggy 的錢。
(A) 瀏覽；(B) 借出；(C) 貸款；(D) **欠 (錢)**

15. 我會永遠珍惜我和好朋友那些年在學校度過的回憶。
(A) 出版；(B) **珍惜**；(C) 改變；(D) 背誦

16. 為什麼警方懷疑 Gina 是兇手？我確定她是無辜的。
(A) 釋放；(B) 提及；(C) **懷疑**；(D) 同意

17. 配備有手電筒，警衛在夜間進行例行巡邏。
(A) **裝備**；(B) 沖馬桶；(C) 使安靜；(D) 擦亮

18. 我覺得電影傳達的訊息是，每個人遲早都要面對死亡。
(A) 翻譯；(B) 搬移；(C) 力勸；(D) **傳達**

19. 打撈隊使用聲納定位沉船。
(A) **找到…的地點**；(B) 治癒；(C) 閃躲；(D) 廢除

20. 地球是環繞太陽旋轉的行星之一。
(A) 垃圾桶；(B) 公克；(C) 資料庫；(D) **行星**

## II. Fill in the Blank

| 1. attention | 2. identify | 3. position |
|---|---|---|
| 4. blocked | 5. possession | |

1. 注意到 Marcus 直視著前方放空，老師走向他並要他專心。
★ pay attention (to sth) 專心；注意

2. 你感同身受主角內心的掙扎嗎？
★ identify with sb/sth 與…產生共鳴

3. 我不是負責人，所以沒有資格發號施令。
★ be in no position to do sth 無資格做某事

4. 我們不該走那條路，因為它被土石流堵住了。
★ block sth up 堵塞，阻塞

5. 梵谷的這幅名畫現在為一位私人收藏家所有。
★ in sb's possession 為某人所有

## III. Guided Translation

1. on; sale
2. Thanks; to
3. right; away
4. in; effect
5. on; average

# Round 16

## I. Multiple Choice

| | | | | |
|---|---|---|---|---|
| 1. C | 2. B | 3. D | 4. A | 5. B |
| 6. A | 7. C | 8. B | 9. B | 10. A |
| 11. D | 12. D | 13. D | 14. C | 15. D |
| 16. D | 17. B | 18. C | 19. A | 20. A |

1. 該國對酒類銷售實施嚴格的限制。
   (A) 描述；(B) 參與者；**(C) 限制**；(D) 指示

2. 收藏家將她貴重的瓷器陳列於玻璃櫃中。
   (A) 小木屋；**(B) 櫥櫃**；(C) 電纜；(D) 自助餐廳

3. 眼不見，心不念。如果你沒有見到某物，你會很容易將其全部遺忘。
   (A) 高度；(B) 騎士；(C) 力量；**(D) 視線**

4. Jasmine 在解那道困難的數學題時搔了頭。
   **(A) 搔**；(B) 戳；(C) 打氣；(D) 遺漏

5. 在說服性寫作中，你必須提供充分合理的論點來支持你的想法。
   (A) 害怕的；**(B) 合乎邏輯的**；(C) 瘋狂的；(D) 擔心的

6. 民眾對於在城市中建造核能發電廠的危險性有所警覺。
   **(A) 警覺的**；(B) 注意到；(C) 膽小的；(D) 統計的

7. 早晨一杯黑咖啡使 Zoe 能夠整天保持清醒。
   (A) 考慮；(B) 申請；**(C) 保持**；(D) 放棄

8. 這些學生的測驗成績反映出他們很認真讀書。
   (A) 供給；**(B) 反映出**；(C) 使安心；(D) 回覆

9. 你不該期望任何奇蹟。只有透過努力成功才會到來。
   (A) 飛彈；**(B) 奇蹟**；(C) 謎團；(D) 導師

10. 那個男孩跌倒傷及左膝，所以他的母親用繃帶包紮它。
    **(A) 繃帶**；(B) 蓋子；(C) 磚頭；(D) 圓錐體

11. 為了殺死害蟲，農民每兩個月在作物上噴灑農藥。
    (A) 染色；(B) 乾燥；(C) 摔碎；**(D) 噴灑**

12. 該問題在董事會會議上引起了激烈的爭論。
    (A) 部屬；(B) 監管；(C) 聲明；**(D) 爭論**

13. 預言家對於世界末日的看法在我看來是一派胡言。我一個字都不信。
    (A) 邏輯；(B) 證據；(C) 情況；**(D) 胡言**

14. 那位勇敢的消防員冒著生命危險拯救困在坍塌建築裡的人。
    (A) 可恥的；(B) 可疑的；**(C) 勇敢的**；(D) 非營利的

15. 火山於昨天爆發了。因此，鄰近村莊被灰燼壟罩。
    (A) 瀑布；(B) 情況；(C) 保證；**(D) 火山**

16. Ben 的雙親都是音樂家。因此，他很早接觸到音樂。
    (A) 錄製；(B) 觸碰；(C) 隱瞞；**(D) 使接觸**

17. 我只是做了些總體的評論。別當成是在針對你個人，否則你會沮喪。
    (A) 私下地；**(B) 個人地**；(C) 突然地；(D) 大約地

18. 那些在外面鳴叫的鳥兒黎明時把我吵醒了。
    (A) 重擊；(B) 轟鳴；**(C) 鳴叫**；(D) 搖擺

19. 在流行音樂會上，觀眾驚訝地注視著這位意外的嘉賓。
    **(A) 注視**；(B) 管理；(C) 提名；(D) 溶解

20. 這種蝴蝶非原生於本地區。牠們來自南美洲。
    **(A) 原生的**；(B) 傳奇的；(C) 次要的；(D) 可行的

## II. Fill in the Blank

| | | |
|---|---|---|
| 1. serves | 2. ride | 3. peak |
| 4. element | 5. impression | |

1. 客廳也作為我們吃飯的空間。
   ★ serve as 當作…用

2. 現在很晚了。你可以載我去火車站嗎？
   ★ give sb a ride 載某人一程

3. 要在旅遊高峰期訂機票不容易。
   ★ at the peak of sth 在…的高峰期

4. Jimmy 的故事有點真實性。他所言的一小部分是真的。★ an element of sth 少量；有點

5. Mindy 以為 Grace 為政府組織工作。
   ★ be under the impression 以為是

## III. Guided Translation

1. all; at; once
2. Provided/Providing; that
3. take; place
4. as; soon; as; possible
5. In; contrast; with

# Round 17

## I. Multiple Choice

| | | | | |
|---|---|---|---|---|
| 1. C | 2. D | 3. A | 4. D | 5. C |
| 6. A | 7. A | 8. B | 9. D | 10. B |
| 11. D | 12. C | 13. A | 14. D | 15. C |
| 16. D | 17. C | 18. B | 19. D | 20. A |

1. 從事勞動工作的人通常必須靠體力幹活。
   (A) 外部的；(B) 危險的；**(C) 體力的**；(D) 精細的

2. 這些藝術品代表了當地藝術家的才華和創造力。
   (A) 敘述的；(B) 嫉妒的；(C) 明智的；**(D) 有代表性的**

3. 保險代理人沒有回我電話。我不認為她真心想幫我。
   **(A) 真誠的**；(B) 易碎的；(C) 欺騙的；(D) 糟透的

4. 這家網路商店保證提供價格划算的高品質產品。
   (A) 推薦；(B) 忽略；(C) 諂媚；**(D) 保證**

5. Joe 的父母給他如此少的零用錢，以至於他得打工賺外快。
   (A) 慶祝會；(B) 專輯；**(C) 零用錢**；(D) 化石

6. 晚餐後，Sophia 喜歡和她丈夫沿著湖邊走走。
   **(A) 岸邊**；(B) 檔案；(C) 雜務；(D) 強盜

7. 臺灣夏天非常炎熱潮濕，尤其是七月和八月。
   **(A) 潮濕的**；(B) 黃銅的；(C) 內疚的；(D) 溫和的

8. 那個男孩眼神充滿淘氣地對他的同學惡作劇。
   (A) 道德觀；**(B) 淘氣**；(C) 同情；(D) 放鬆

9. 讓我們為這對新婚伴侶敬酒！
   (A) 報告；(B) 中風；(C) 盛宴；**(D) 敬酒**

10. Sam 無法分辨不同顏色。他是色盲。
    (A) 討厭；**(B) 分辨**；(C) 分發；(D) 擾亂

11. 年幼的孩子對周圍的事物充滿好奇並不斷提出問題是很正常的。
    (A) 習慣性的；(B) 獨特的；(C) 傳統的；**(D) 正常的**

12. 衛生部長在疫情期間於每日下午兩點向全國直播。
    (A) 探索；(B) 寫程式；**(C) 廣播**；(D) 鼓勵

13. 伴隨著洗衣機的發明，人們可以輕鬆洗衣服。
    **(A) 待洗衣物**；(B) 救生員；(C) 真空；(D) 退休金

14. 絕對不要以犧牲安全為代價來追求獲利。
    (A) 擴展；(B) 探險；(C) 經驗；**(D) 代價**

15. 植物在白天產生氧氣幫助淨化人類呼吸的空氣。
    (A) 荒地；(B) 監護；**(C) 氧氣**；(D) 濕氣

16. 我在派對上誤認 Molly 為她的妹妹，因為她們有驚人的相似之處。
    (A) 商業的；(B) 潛在的；(C) 結實的；**(D) 驚人的**

17. 在我去學校的路上，我看到一群工人在修路。
    (A) 槍；(B) 口香糖；**(C) 群**；(D) 穀物

18. 為了擁有健康的寶寶，女性被建議懷孕期間停止飲酒和抽菸。
    (A) 頻率；**(B) 懷孕**；(C) 空缺；(D) 精確

19. Emily 每月以信用卡支付她的保險費。
    (A) 被告人；(B) 風格；(C) 意識形態；**(D) 保險費**

20. 對 Fred 來說，要說服他固執的爸爸改變心意是具有挑戰性的任務。
    **(A) 說服**；(B) 交談；(C) 對照；(D) 傳達

## II. Fill in the Blank

| | | |
|---|---|---|
| 1. pick | 2. caught | 3. mess |
| 4. pride | 5. fear | |

1. 為什麼你總是找我麻煩。我受夠了！
   ★ pick on sb 對⋯刁難

2. Elliot 肯定也感冒了，因為他的症狀和你的一樣。★ catch a cold 感冒

3. A：我週末可以借你的車嗎？
   B：當然不要！你總是把我的車弄得一團糟。
   ★ make a mess of sth 把⋯弄糟、搞砸

4. 這對老夫婦為兒子的成就感到驕傲。
   ★ take pride in sb/sth 為⋯驕傲

5. Rowan 不敢告訴他父親這個消息，生怕他會勃然大怒。★ for fear that/of sth 生怕，以免

## III. Guided Translation

1. give; call
2. in; case; of
3. gone; from; bad; to; worse
4. takes; delight; in
5. came; up; with

# Round 18

## I. Multiple Choice

| | | | | |
|---|---|---|---|---|
| 1. A | 2. D | 3. D | 4. A | 5. B |
| 6. B | 7. A | 8. C | 9. A | 10. D |
| 11. D | 12. A | 13. B | 14. D | 15. C |
| 16. A | 17. C | 18. B | 19. C | 20. D |

1. 該飯店生意在傳染病爆發後倒閉。
   (A) **(企業) 失敗**；(B) 爆裂；(C) 豎起；(D) 跳傘

2. 每當 Theo 閱讀時，他會在書頁空白處寫下評語。
   (A) 白色衣服；(B) 洞察力；(C) 瘀傷；**(D) 書頁空白處**

3. 英文寫作的基本架構和中文寫作不同。
   (A) 展覽；(B) 大成功；(C) 珠寶；**(D) 架構**

4. 整個國家都在為戰爭中士兵的死亡哀悼。
   **(A) 哀悼**；(B) 相信；(C) 緩解；(D) 欺騙

5. 該劇情節和《哈姆雷特》有些相似之處。它們都是關於一名王子向父親的兇手復仇。
   (A) 臨時工作；**(B) 相似處**；(C) 標準；(D) 品質

6. 這高爾夫球手在 23 歲仍為業餘者而非職業選手時贏得錦標賽。
   (A) 代理商；**(B) 業餘者**；(C) 積極分子；(D) 管理者

7. Lauren 在進入娛樂產業前曾是一名法律執業者。她曾代表客戶出庭。
   **(A) 執業者**；(B) 感應器；(C) 拓荒者；(D) 奴隸

8. 該組織是在幫助那些遭受家暴的悲慘兒童。
   (A) 意外的；(B) 很棒的；**(C) 悲慘的**；(D) 足夠的

9. 這個研究證實了一個假設，有吃早餐的學生表現得比沒吃的學生好。
   **(A) 假設**；(B) 論壇；(C) 資料夾；(D) 贊助

10. 門階上站著一名銀髮男子。你知道他是誰嗎？
    (A) 很瘦的；(B) 沉默的；(C) 陰涼的；**(D) 銀色的**

11. 那名心碎的女子和她丈夫離婚，因為他吸毒且沒有穩定的工作。
    (A) 消化；(B) 求婚；(C) 訂婚；**(D) 離婚**

12. 我總是把筆和紙放在手邊，這樣我就可以在需要的時候做筆記。
    **(A) 筆記**；(B) 告示；(C) 著作；(D) 回覆

13. 該名老師因為痛毆他的學生而被起訴。
    (A) 軟弱的；**(B) 殘暴的**；(C) 慢性的；(D) 溫柔的

14. 我們自從高中畢業後就沒 Miranda 的消息了。
    (A) 猶豫；(B) 凝視；(C) 保持；**(D) 畢業**

15. 聖誕樹周圍放著幾個包裝精美的包裹。
    (A) 香腸；(B) 人質；**(C) 包裹**；(D) 補丁

16. Tobby 唱獨唱的部分，樂隊其他成員則在副歌加入。
    **(A) 副歌**；(B) 管弦樂團；(C) 症狀；(D) 房間

17. 天氣太熱了，那名馬拉松選手流了很多汗。
    (A) 結婚；(B) 吸取；**(C) 流汗**；(D) 漂浮

18. 該國的貧富差距很大。
    (A) 單腳跳；**(B) 差距**；(C) 輕觸；(D) 啜飲

19. 在冰箱發明之前，人們會以陽光曬乾或用鹽浸漬來保存食物。
    (A) 保留；(B) 取得；**(C) 保存**；(D) 反對

20. 小孩在萬聖節穿盛裝去收集糖果是一種習俗。
    (A) 廢墟；(B) 翻譯；(C) 橡皮水管；**(D) 服裝**

## II. Fill in the Blank

| | | |
|---|---|---|
| 1. emphasis | 2. balance | 3. inferior |
| 4. compare | 5. commanded | |

1. 我的老師很重視講英文的能力。因此，我們經常在課堂上練習說英文。
   ★ put emphasis on sth 重視某物

2. 我們必須在揮霍無度與省吃儉用之間取得平衡。★ strike a balance (between) 取得平衡

3. 一般來說，即溶咖啡口感不如現磨咖啡。這就是為何它較為便宜。
   ★ inferior 較差的，次等的

4. 根據希臘神話，Helen 的美貌是無與倫比的。甚至連女神們都忌妒她的美麗。
   ★ beyond compare 無與倫比

5. 這些步兵在戰爭中與敵人對抗時，被命令不要

投降。★ command 命令

## III. Guided Translation

1. comes; into; use
2. passed; away
3. take; the; risk; of
4. take; rain; check
5. come; into; effect

# Round 19

## I. Multiple Choice

| | | | | |
|---|---|---|---|---|
| 1. B | 2. D | 3. B | 4. A | 5. D |
| 6. C | 7. D | 8. C | 9. D | 10. A |
| 11. A | 12. A | 13. C | 14. B | 15. B |
| 16. D | 17. B | 18. C | 19. C | 20. A |

1. Freya 總會把所有困擾她的事情都告訴她親密的朋友。
   (A) 可選擇的；(B) **親密的**；(C) 歷史的；(D) 瑣碎的

2. 這條法律的目的是消除工作環境的性別不平等。
   (A) 增加；(B) 清空；(C) 調查；(D) **消除**

3. 此醫學實驗涉及一些哈佛大學和牛津大學等頂尖大學的合作。
   (A) 津貼；(B) **合作**；(C) 特銷經營權；(D) 虧損

4. 搭乘航空的旅客必須把行李放在座位下或頭上的置物櫃。
   (A) **行李**；(B) 帳戶；(C) 碎片；(D) 通道

5. 那名女士在有人闖入她房子時受到驚嚇，並害怕得僵住不動
   (A) 失望的；(B) 開心的；(C) 扭曲的；(D) **驚嚇的**

6. 多名志願者抵達戰火前線無私地給予幫助。
   (A) 雕像；(B) 機器人；(C) **志願者**；(D) 房東

7. Ruby 在國王街新開的美髮廳剪髮和染髮。
   (A) 古柯鹼；(B) 標準；(C) 垃圾桶；(D) **美髮廳**

8. 你嘲笑別人的不幸很不友善。
   (A) 不在場；(B) 幽默；(C) **不幸**；(D) 成功

9. 這件絲質襯衫特價四折，真的很便宜。
   (A) 流質；(B) 地產；(C) 娛樂；(D) **便宜貨**

10. 我幾分鐘前有看到 Roger。他現在一定在大樓某處。
    (A) **在某處**；(B) 稍微有點；(C) 不知為何；(D) 有時

11. 古羅馬人曾一度主宰歐洲。他們掌控了整個大陸的很大一部分。
    (A) **主宰**；(B) 毀壞；(C) 重建；(D) 建立

12. 現今的生活費用更高，所以很難將支出控制在預算內。
    (A) **預算**；(B) 基金；(C) 農業；(D) 投機活動

13. Sophie 用五句話概述這個童話故事。
    (A) 偵查；(B) 成功；(C) **概述**；(D) 支持

14. 園丁正在用一副大剪刀修剪灌木叢。
    (A) 一張；(B) **一副**；(C) 一對；(D) 霹靂聲

15. 這個噩耗很快就傳遍了整個城鎮。
    (A) 選舉；(B) **傳遞**；(C) 擴大；(D) 抵達

16. 消防隊員努力阻止火勢蔓延。
    (A) 使能夠；(B) 庇護；(C) 貢獻；(D) **蔓延**

17. 近年來，政府減少日本汽車的進口配額，以推動本土汽車業。
    (A) 圖示；(B) **配額**；(C) 圈，環；(D) 場地

18. 隨著期末考的到來，學生們面臨著讀完所有考試的巨大壓力。
    (A) 力量；(B) 政權；(C) **壓力**；(D) 寬慰

19. 香菸煙霧總讓我咳嗽，所以我盡量遠離吸菸者。
    (A) 模仿；(B) 打草稿；(C) **咳嗽**；(D) 笑

20. Ian 指控 Amber 在網路發布關於他的不實謠言。
    (A) **不實的**；(B) 同樣的；(C) 塑膠的；(D) 合法的

## II. Fill in the Blank

| | | |
|---|---|---|
| 1. committed | 2. stealing | 3. infected |
| 4. concentrate | 5. reached | |

1. 那名女子犯下重罪，並在獄中度過餘生。
   ★ commit a crime 犯罪

2. 那名白領工作者今早被指控偷她同事的錢。
   ★ accuse sb of (doing) sth 指控某人做某事

3. 大多數當地居民都感染了某種細菌，其中一人甚至生命垂危。★ infect 感染

4. 如果你想通過英文能力檢定，你必須專注於練習你的聽力技巧。★ concentrate 專心

5. 雙方最終達成協定。該司機需賠償車禍受害人新臺幣 5 萬元。★ reach a settlement 達成協定

## III. Guided Translation

1. pay; off
2. rain; or; shine
3. physically; abused
4. put; into; practice
5. based; on

# Round 20

## I. Multiple Choice

| | | | | |
|---|---|---|---|---|
| 1. D | 2. D | 3. A | 4. A | 5. B |
| 6. B | 7. A | 8. D | 9. C | 10. C |
| 11. B | 12. B | 13. C | 14. C | 15. A |
| 16. D | 17. C | 18. B | 19. A | 20. D |

1. 老闆要求助理按字母順序存放客戶的檔案。
   (A) 容器；(B) 嬰兒；(C) 預言家；**(D) 助理**

2. 請勿將合約內容透露給他人。我們必須保密。
   (A) 爭搶；(B) 期待；(C) 折磨；**(D) 透露**

3. Ted 的夾克和我的很相似。它們都是深藍色。
   **(A) 相似的**；(B) 熟悉的；(C) 有關聯的；(D) 明顯的

4. 快！叫救護車！我認為那男子心臟病發作了。
   **(A) 救護車**；(B) 公告；(C) 耳機；(D) 扳機

5. Susan 是火車事故中唯一的生還者。火車上的其他乘客都罹難了。
   (A) 受害者；**(B) 生還者**；(C) 爭論；(D) 興奮

6. Sullivan 女士是一位虔誠的基督徒，她過著遵從基督教教義的生活。
   (A) 禮節；**(B) 遵從**；(C) 奴隸；(D) 脾氣

7. 對 Sam 來說，害怕與陌生人交談是他交新朋友的最大障礙。
   **(A) 障礙**；(B) 情緒；(C) 年輕人；(D) 機長

8. Ray 在夜市吃了不乾淨的食物，不久後胃部不適。
   (A) 鼻子；(B) 肺；(C) 肝；**(D) 胃**

9. 因為我沒有戲劇天分，所以我演技很差。
   (A) 民主的；(B) 實際的；**(C) 戲劇的**；(D) 批評的

10. 我的祖父是一個開明的人，對任何新奇的想法總是持開放的態度。
    (A) 惡意的；(B) 自願的；**(C) 新奇的**；(D) 最近的

11. 沒有梯子，Jeffrey 不可能更換天花板上的燈泡。
    (A) 地板；**(B) 燈泡**；(C) 地毯；(D) 家具

12. 船要沉了，所以乘客們迅速穿上救生衣。
    (A) 踢；**(B) 下沉**；(C) 騙局；(D) 眨眼

13. 這個年輕的女孩常常幻想自己是走在伸展臺上的時裝模特兒。
    (A) 領導；(B) 連接；**(C) 想像**；(D) 使困惑

14. 所有的斑馬一看到獅群正在靠近便驚慌地逃跑。
    (A) 快樂；(B) 耐心；**(C) 驚慌**；(D) 悲傷

15. 要不是你的警告，我會在股市損失一大筆錢。
    **(A) 警告**；(B) 感謝；(C) 詛咒；(D) 刻板印象

16. 有些醫師不贊成僅有蔬果的飲食。
    (A) 反對；(B) 反抗；(C) 暫停；**(D) 皺眉**

17. Ben 下定決心要贏得比賽，沒有什麼能阻止他實現自己的目標。
    (A) 克服；(B) 反對；**(C) 阻止**；(D) 防衛

18. 今年第三季度的銷售額大致符合他們的預期。
    (A) 回覆；**(B) 相當於**；(C) 奉獻；(D) 公開譴責

19. 那名政治人物的行為與他的話不一致。
    **(A) 一致的**；(B) 中立的；(C) 有可能的；(D) 誠實的

20. Cindy 察覺到一路上有名男子跟著自己，連忙跑進最近的一間便利商店。
    (A) 憐憫的；(B) 尷尬的；(C) 市政的；**(D) 意識到的**

## II. Fill in the Blank

| | | |
|---|---|---|
| 1. informed | 2. record | 3. worn |
| 4. roll | 5. instant | |

1. 讓我了解股票價格變化的情況。不要讓我錯過賺大錢的機會。
   ★ keep sb informed of sth 讓某人了解某事

2. 科學家們每天記錄地球的活動。
   ★ keep a record 做紀錄

3. 密集訓練已經使棒球選手們精疲力盡。
   ★ wear sb out 使某人筋疲力盡

4. 老師點名看誰今天早上缺席。
   ★ call the roll 點名

5. 那名通緝犯一看到警察就跑了。
★ the instant (that) 一…就…

## III. Guided Translation

1. lost; touch; with
2. put; up; with
3. in; no; time
4. set; up
5. end; up

# Round 21

## I. Multiple Choice

| 1. D | 2. A | 3. D | 4. A | 5. B |
|------|------|------|------|------|
| 6. C | 7. D | 8. C | 9. A | 10. C |
| 11. C | 12. B | 13. C | 14. D | 15. B |
| 16. B | 17. D | 18. A | 19. B | 20. A |

1. 觀眾對於昨晚馬戲團表演的雜技感到驚奇。
(A) 將…減到最低；(B) 擠出；(C) 明白；**(D) 使吃驚**

2. 當工作及時完成時，我的主管和同事們都鬆了一口氣。
**(A) 同事**；(B) 指揮；(C) 作曲家；(D) 收藏家

3. 大夜班員工從半夜工作到清晨。
(A) 方法；(B) 遺產；(C) 條件；**(D) 輪班**

4. 你不能把車停在這個區域。它保留給殘障人士使用。
**(A) 保留**；(B) 出現；(C) 劈開；(D) 融化

5. 這位富裕的名人擁有許多奢侈品，例如珠寶和名牌包。
(A) 代理人；**(B) 奢侈**；(C) 貨幣；(D) 社區

6. 分析完情況後，我們對下一步該做什麼有了清楚的想法。
(A) 填塞；(B) 做出結論；**(C) 分析**；(D) 補救

7. 新娘的大鑽戒在陽光下閃閃發光。
(A) 開槍；(B) 震驚；(C) 關閉；**(D) 閃耀**

8. Liam 總是從羅伯特‧佛洛斯特寫的詩中獲得靈感。
(A) 介紹；(B) 安裝；**(C) 靈感**；(D) 指示

9. 當 Steve 回到家時，他發現他的房子被闖入，所有金手錶都不見了。
**(A) 丟失的**；(B) 進行中的；(C) 有前途的；(D) 狡

猾的

10. 清潔人員在清洗拖把後，將髒水倒進水溝裡。
(A) 指派；(B) 殺害；**(C) 倒 (液體)**；(D) 埋葬

11. Karen 在實施節儉運動，她正盡最大努力減少開支。
(A) 敵意；(B) 味道；**(C) 有計畫的努力**；(D) 案例

12. 大眾仍然關注核電廠可能對環境造成的負面影響。
(A) 原產的；**(B) 核能的**；(C) 有營養的；(D) 狹窄的

13. 鎮民舉辦遊行，以慶祝棒球隊剛贏得冠軍。
(A) 暴動；(B) 長途健行；**(C) 遊行**；(D) 抗議

14. 情人節那天，Henry 送女友一束紅玫瑰以表達對她的愛。
(A) (有把手的) 桶；(B) 桶子；(C) 瓶；**(D) 束，串**

15. 圖書館裡的書是按學科分類的。
(A) 灑出；**(B) 分類**；(C) 形成；(D) 產生

16. 這名服裝設計師經常閱讀有關最新時尚的雜誌，以讓自己與時俱進。
(A) 最後的；**(B) 最新的**；(C) 稍後的；(D) 後者的

17. 這名企業家以他的方式做任何事。他從不追隨別人的所作所為。
(A) 勝利；(B) 王國；(C) 範圍；**(D) 方式**

18. 我忘記我們在先前的談話中說了什麼。你能幫我重溫一下記憶嗎？
**(A) 先前的**；(B) 首要的；(C) 熱衷的；(D) 悲慘的

19. 每當這名導演感到沮喪時，他就會去鄉下，在樹林裡靜思。
(A) 失敗；**(B) 靜思**；(C) 重複；(D) 威脅

20. 商標為產品創建形象，且可以是個很好的廣告手段。
**(A) 手段**；(B) 供應量；(C) 主題；(D) 休息室

## II. Fill in the Blank

| 1. result | 2. consequence | 3. room |
|-----------|----------------|---------|
| 4. interfere | 5. polish | |

1. 汽車排放廢氣導致空氣汙染。
★ result in sth 導致

2. Harper 今早錯過了校車，結果她上學遲到。
★ in consequence 結果，所以

3. 為了騰出空間給她的新衣服，Melissa 捐了一些

她的舊衣服給當地的慈善機構。
★ make room 騰出空間

4. Martha 干涉鄰居的個人事務是很不明智的。
★ interfere in sth 干涉、介入某事

5. 在我去巴黎旅行之前，我必須加強我的法語。
★ polish up 加強技能，改進

## III. Guided Translation

1. set; off
2. once; again
3. put; out
4. Because; of
5. think; of

# Round 22

## I. Multiple Choice

| | | | | |
|---|---|---|---|---|
| 1. D | 2. B | 3. A | 4. A | 5. C |
| 6. B | 7. A | 8. D | 9. D | 10. A |
| 11. C | 12. D | 13. B | 14. C | 15. D |
| 16. C | 17. A | 18. C | 19. B | 20. D |

1. 有些人認為安裝監視器是侵犯隱私。
   (A) 殘疾；(B) 殘忍；(C) 效率；**(D) 隱私**

2. Ivy 不習慣與陌生人有身體接觸。連握手都會讓她感到不安。
   (A) 產量；**(B) 接觸**；(C) 巡迴；(D) 自尊

3. 新聞報導說，兩名警察和一名罪犯在昨晚的槍擊事件中喪生。
   **(A) 事件**；(B) 集會；(C) 印象；(D) 傳統

4. 人類自古就開始用火。
   **(A) 古代的**；(B) 備用的；(C) 珍貴的；(D) 浪漫的

5. 警察抓住竊賊的手臂，把他帶到警察局。
   (A) 領養；(B) 計畫；**(C) 抓住**；(D) 參加

6. Skyler 把全麥麥片浸入在牛奶中，把它當作早午餐。
   (A) 敲打；**(B) 淹沒**；(C) 喝；(D) 瀝乾

7. 這名修女堅信她一生的使命是幫助窮人。
   **(A) 使命**；(B) 經濟蕭條；(C) 慶祝會；(D) 承認

8. 熊在河中用牠的爪子抓魚。
   (A) 毛皮；(B) 大腿；(C) (細胞) 組織；**(D) 爪子**

9. 每個月底，我的零用錢所剩無幾。
   (A) 嚇人的；(B) 嚴厲的；(C) 安全的；**(D) 缺乏的**

10. 車禍導致公路上的交通中斷了幾個小時。
    **(A) 停止**；(B) 實行；(C) 破壞；(D) 改善

11. 買房通常會帶給年輕夫婦沉重的經濟負擔。
    (A) 包，捆；(B) 子彈；**(C) 負擔**；(D) 局

12. 毒品醜聞對這位參議員的聲譽有毀滅性影響。
    (A) 害怕的；(B) 極好的；(C) 最喜歡的；**(D) 毀滅性的**

13. 法律規定，車內的所有乘客都必須繫上安全帶。
    (A) 外國人；**(B) 乘客**；(C) 從業人員；(D) 外交官

14. 拿起螃蟹時，手指要遠離蟹螯。
    (A) 子句；(B) 拍手聲；**(C) 爪；螯**；(D) 衝突

15. 這位野心勃勃的演員每天長時間工作，冒著健康風險在好萊塢追求名利。
    (A) 郵資；(B) 報告；(C) 洞察力；**(D) 追求**

16. 披薩看起來太好吃了，Mark 無法抗拒誘惑咬了一口。
    (A) 幫助；(B) 堅稱；**(C) 抗拒 (誘惑等)**；(D) 堅持

17. 小時候，媽媽經常透過寓言和童話故事教導我誠實的美德。
    **(A) 誠實**；(B) 緊張；(C) 功能；(D) 參加

18. 人們應該要有勇氣捍衛自己的信念。
    (A) 拒絕；(B) 創造力；**(C) 勇氣**；(D) 感激

19. 諷刺的是，人類發明了機器讓生活更輕鬆，但最終卻過著更加忙碌的生活。
    (A) 行為；**(B) 機器**；(C) 地平線；(D) 攝影

20. 只有一些人住在那偏遠的島嶼上。人口約 3000 人。
    (A) 宣布；(B) 娛樂；(C) 限制；**(D) 人口**

## II. Fill in the Blank

| | | |
|---|---|---|
| 1. willing | 2. headlines | 3. content |
| 4. width | 5. lesson | |

1. 強震發生後，這群志工願意提供協助。
   ★ be willing (to do sth) 願意做某事

2. 女王逝世的消息一出，馬上成為該國的頭條新聞。★ make (the) headlines 登上報紙頭條新聞

3. 我對我現在的工作很滿意。我暫時不想換工

作。★ content with sth 對某件事感到滿意

4. 我們學校前面的路寬 5 公尺。★ in width 寬

5. Ellie 已經記取教訓。 我希望她不要再做蠢事了。★ learn a/your lesson 記取教訓

## III. Guided Translation

1. pull; down
2. bear; in; mind
3. bed; of; roses
4. effort; put; into
5. lost; sight; of

# Round 23

## I. Multiple Choice

| | | | | |
|---|---|---|---|---|
| 1. B | 2. B | 3. D | 4. C | 5. C |
| 6. D | 7. B | 8. A | 9. C | 10. A |
| 11. C | 12. A | 13. B | 14. B | 15. A |
| 16. D | 17. D | 18. A | 19. C | 20. D |

1. 由於政治和宗教信仰不同，這對夫妻的婚姻以離婚告終。
   (A) 開水壺；(B) **信仰**；(C) 睡衣褲；(D) 峭壁

2. 昨晚的大地震是我們經歷過的最大災難。
   (A) 可忍受的；(B) **巨大的**；(C) 耳聾的；(D) 精神的

3. Joanna 回到家時，惱怒地發現她的公事包遺落在公車上。
   (A) 凌亂的；(B) 通常的；(C) 可怕的；(D) **惱怒的**

4. 「運輸」一詞有四個音節，我們用重音讀第三音節。
   (A) 暗喻；(B) 發音；(C) **音節**；(D) 分數

5. 現在草莓夠熟，我們可以摘下來了。
   (A) 罕見的；(B) 精確的；(C) **成熟的**；(D) 必要的

6. 開發中國家很難在工業發展和環境保護之間取得平衡。
   (A) 可相比的；(B) 最終的；(C) 交替的；(D) **工業的**

7. Roy 先生正在申請綠卡以成為美國的永久居民。
   (A) 具體的；(B) **永久的**；(C) 激烈的；(D) 有毒的

8. 許多當地居民聚集在市政廳，與市長面對面交談。

(A) **大廳**；(B) 通行費；(C) 洋娃娃；(D) 掉落

9. Green 小姐今早在公園被搶了錢包。她的損失包含一百美元和兩張信用卡。
   (A) 辨別；(B) 有資格；(C) **搶劫**；(D) 否認

10. 那名瓦斯氣爆的目擊者嚇得目瞪口呆。他有幾分鐘沒辦法說出話來。
    (A) **說不出話來的**；(B) 不同的；(C) 虔誠的；(D) 泥濘的

11. 你認為讓學生在任何情況下都絕對服從，不提出任何異議，這樣好嗎？
    (A) 無罪的；(B) 有系統的；(C) **服從的**；(D) 數學的

12. 一進淋浴間， William 迅速地解開了襯衫的釦子。
    (A) **鈕扣**；(B) 衣領；(C) 袖子；(D) 口袋

13. Alvin 買的皮外套花了新臺幣兩萬三千元。 幾乎是我月薪的一半。
    (A) 墮胎；(B) **薪水**；(C) 硬體；(D) 身分

14. 結果顯示有五十票贊成該法案，三票反對。
    (A) 表情；(B) **贊成**；(C) 榮譽；(D) 風景

15. Monica 從不表達自己的想法，只是被動地接受任何提供給她的東西。
    (A) **被動地**；(B) 樂觀地；(C) 活躍地；(D) 認真地

16. 我們認為 Richard 頭腦很好，因為他有一個聰明的計畫來幫助我們擺脫困境。
    (A) 偏僻的；(B) 愚蠢的；(C) 乏味的；(D) **聰明的**

17. 商業廣告的目的是抓住消費者的注意力，讓他們對產品感興趣。
    (A) 顧問；(B) 經濟學家；(C) (大學) 講師；(D) **消費者**

18. Sara 正在節食，但是蛋糕看起來很誘人，她想吃一塊。
    (A) **誘人的**；(B) 粗魯的；(C) 辛辣的；(D) 昏昏欲睡的

19. 學生們被要求反覆排練這齣戲，直到他們的表演達到完美。
    (A) 保險；(B) 保證；(C) **表演**；(D) 容忍

20. 大多國會議員投票反對增加軍事預算，因為他們認為不久的將來不會有任何戰爭威脅。
    (A) 憲法允許的；(B) 農業的；(C) 聯邦政府的；(D) **軍事的**

## II. Fill in the Blank

| 1. breath | 2. involved | 3. excels |
|---|---|---|
| 4. names | 5. dressed | |

1. 我發現跟那個固執的男子講道理簡直是白費唇舌。★ waste your breath 白費唇舌

2. 那名罪犯因參與搶劫被送進監獄。
   ★ involved 使參與，牽涉

3. Leo 擅長跑步。他是學校裡跑得最快的。
   ★ excel in sth 擅長某事

4. 你那樣辱罵他是不好的。畢竟，他是你的兄弟。★ call sb names 辱罵…

5. 這位女士盛裝出席皇室宴會，卻發現忘記帶邀請函。★ dress up 盛裝

## III. Guided Translation

1. once; and; for; all
2. seems; to
3. great; deal; of
4. On; the; contrary
5. put; on; weight

# Round 24

## I. Multiple Choice

| 1. A | 2. C | 3. C | 4. D | 5. A |
|---|---|---|---|---|
| 6. C | 7. B | 8. A | 9. D | 10. D |
| 11. C | 12. D | 13. D | 14. A | 15. B |
| 16. B | 17. B | 18. A | 19. B | 20. C |

1. 這位年老患者沒有正確吞嚥食物，結果被噎住了。
   (A) **正確地**；(B) 突出地；(C) 粗糙地；(D) 感激地

2. 這名野心勃勃的男子拋棄他的家人去追求名聲及財富。
   (A) 拒絕；(B) 拋棄；(C) **追求**；(D) 用拳猛擊

3. 你可以從飯店房間的窗戶看到遠處群山和下方美麗湖泊的壯麗景色。
   (A) 體貼的；(B) 熱衷的；(C) **壯觀的**；(D) 謹慎的

4. 隨著大學入學考試的到來，Leo 心中充滿焦慮。
   (A) 獲得；(B) 拒絕；(C) 大理石；(D) **焦慮**

5. 房間裡的每個人感覺到地面在震動，都驚恐地尖叫起來。
   (A) **尖叫**；(B) 搔，抓；(C) 捨棄；(D) 刷洗

6. 因為高通貨膨脹，所有東西都比上個月貴了一倍。
   (A) 勤勉；(B) 自私；(C) **通貨膨脹**；(D) 吸引力

7. 我們只能住普通的旅館。豪華的我們無法負擔。
   (A) 現代的；(B) **普通的**；(C) 中間的；(D) 紀念的

8. 你有聽到我們帳篷外蟋蟀發出的聲音嗎？
   (A) **帳篷**；(B) 緣故；(C) 嘉年華會；(D) 野獸

9. 這家店販售各種各樣的帽子。你總能找到你想要的帽子。
   (A) 建築物；(B) 裝飾；(C) 考試；(D) **可供挑選的東西**

10. Emily 在機場得為她的香水和烈酒繳納關稅。
    (A) 便條紙；(B) 處罰；(C) 遊行；(D) **稅金**

11. 記者最重要的是客觀報導事實，而不是對別人加以評判。
    (A) 保護的；(B) 活躍的；(C) **客觀的**；(D) 易爆炸的

12. 蜜蜂在花園的花朵之間嗡嗡作響。
    (A) 逃走；(B) 分析；(C) 清掃；(D) **嗡嗡作響**

13. 沒有人願意和這個自私的女孩做朋友，因為她只關心自己。
    (A) 有影響力的；(B) 很棒的；(C) 繁榮的；(D) **自私的**

14. Max 打籃球時扭傷腳踝，醫生讓他休息一週。
    (A) **腳踝**；(B) 熱帶叢林；(C) 時刻表；(D) 泡沫

15. 如果你去國外旅行，你應該隨身攜帶護照。
    (A) 可能性；(B) **護照**；(C) 害蟲；(D) 乘客

16. 襄理被指派在今天下午兩點與一位新客戶簽合約。
    (A) 病患；(B) **客戶**；(C) 收件人；(D) 遊客

17. 我反對打獵，因為這違背了我尊重所有生物的原則。
    (A) 校長；(B) **原則**；(C) 潛力；(D) 降落傘

18. 不要隨身攜帶太多現金。你可以開一個儲蓄帳戶，然後把錢存到銀行。
    (A) **儲蓄**；(B) 運動員；(C) 調整；(D) 啟程

19. 學生對教授的寶貴指導表示由衷的感謝。
    (A) 鑿子；(B) **感謝**；(C) 亞麻；(D) 歌劇

20. 孩子們正在看一隻毛毛蟲爬上花莖。
　　(A) 挖掘；(B) 偷偷溜走；**(C) 爬行**；(D) 拉長

## II. Fill in the Blank

| | | |
|---|---|---|
| 1. isolated | 2. exposed | 3. response |
| 4. longing | 5. traffic | |

1. 得了流感的孩子必須與家裡其他健康的孩子隔開。★ isolate 使隔離

2. 士兵們暴露在危險之中。他們沒有受到保護。★ expose sb to sth 使某人暴露於 (險境)

3. 政府沒有採取任何行動來回應人們對市區惡劣交通的抱怨。★ in response to 回應

4. 兩國經過多年的戰爭後，雙方人民都渴望和平。★ long for sth 渴望…

5. 大城市的上下班尖峰時間總是會塞車。★ traffic jam 交通堵塞

## III. Guided Translation

1. ran; across
2. by; no; means
3. free; of
4. on; way
5. gave; birth; to

# Round 25

## I. Multiple Choice

| | | | | |
|---|---|---|---|---|
| 1. D | 2. A | 3. C | 4. B | 5. A |
| 6. D | 7. C | 8. A | 9. D | 10. B |
| 11. B | 12. C | 13. D | 14. A | 15. D |
| 16. B | 17. C | 18. A | 19. B | 20. C |

1. 家長們力勸當局立刻採取行動，阻止病毒在兒童間進一步擴散。
　　(A) 確保；(B) 統治；(C) 承認；**(D) 力勸**

2. 那兩隊在爭奪國際數學奧林匹亞競賽金牌。
　　**(A) 獎牌**；(B) 全體演員陣容；(C) 領帶；(D) 禮服

3. 維持自然界的平衡非常重要，這樣所有生物才能生存。
　　(A) 玷汙；(B) 包含；**(C) 維持**；(D) 娛樂

4. 205 次列車將誤點 30 分鐘，車站人員對帶來的不便深表歉意。
　　(A) 同意；**(B) 道歉**；(C) 擔心；(D) 跌倒

5. 別開玩笑了。你怎麼能指望別人在你每次犯錯的時候都原諒你呢？
　　**(A) 可笑的**；(B) 有關聯的；(C) 悲觀的；(D) 密集的

6. Louis 希望成為一名游泳教練，教人如何游泳。
　　(A) 酗酒者；(B) 候選人；(C) 馬戲團；**(D) 教練**

7. 我認為 Jay 應該學著謙虛地對待他的成就。覺得比別人優越沒有多高尚。
　　(A) 自信的；(B) 幽默的；**(C) 謙虛的**；(D) 小心的

8. 難民們乞求國際援助組織的幫助。
　　**(A) 乞求**；(B) 闡明；(C) 舀出；(D) 密謀

9. Theo 大致上是這麼說的。其實，我不是很確定。
　　(A) 逐漸地；(B) 悲慘地；(C) 苗條地；**(D) 大致地**

10. 這件外套是用非常耐用的材料製成的。它可以穿好幾年。
　　(A) 共同的；**(B) 耐用的**；(C) 僅僅的；(D) 政治的

11. 由於經濟不景氣，我們公司似乎不可能實現銷售額增長 10% 的目標。
　　(A) 給予知識的；**(B) 經濟的**；(C) 比較的；(D) 行政的

12. 這位職業運動員歷經千辛萬苦才得以揚名。
　　(A) 賭場；(B) 論文；**(C) 苦難**；(D) (棒球的) 局

13. 那間公司聘請了幾名兼職人員在街上分發免費的洗髮精試用品。
　　(A) 講座；(B) 廟宇；(C) 餐巾紙；**(D) 試用品**

14. 這款掃地機器人的一個重要特點是它能偵測房裡骯髒的區域。
　　**(A) 特點**；(B) 路徑；(C) 努力；(D) 例子

15. 我們要有密碼才能存取電腦上的機密文件。
　　(A) 消遣；(B) 熱愛；(C) 毒藥；**(D) 密碼**

16. 那名單親爸爸非常努力地工作以供給三個小孩吃穿。
　　(A) 把…歸因於…；**(B) 為…提供衣服**；(C) (尤指出庭) 作證；(D) (公開) 贊同

17. 在法庭上，每個人都應享有平等的權利；沒有人可以享受任何特權。
　　(A) 支持；(B) 幻想；**(C) 特權**；(D) 利潤

18. 機上所有人都在墜機事件中喪生，包含駕駛員、乘客和機組人員。

(A) **(船、飛機的) 全體工作人員**；(B) 烏鴉；(C) 咀嚼物；(D) 群眾

19. Gary 現金花光了，於是在超商的自動櫃員機提領了新臺幣五千元。
(A) 存款；**(B) 提款**；(C) 打擾；(D) 想出

20. 你能仔細描述搶匪的長相嗎？
(A) 開藥；(B) 使分心；**(C) 描述**；(D) 襲擊

## II. Fill in the Blank

| | | |
|---|---|---|
| 1. count | 2. worth | 3. blamed |
| 4. gearing | 5. course | |

1. 當你有需要的時候，你都可以依靠我。
   ★ count on sb 依靠…

2. 在頒獎典禮上，這位女演員身穿黑色晚禮服，佩戴價值約美金十五萬元的鑽石項鍊。
   ★ worth 值 (多少) 錢的

3. 那些粗心的露營者因引發森林大火而備受指責。★ blame 歸咎於

4. 邁阿密海灘的旅遊酒店都在為即將到來的假期做準備。★ gear (sb/sth) up 準備

5. 在面試的過程中，漸漸可以看出該應徵者不適合此職。★ in the course of 在…期間

## III. Guided Translation

1. under; protest
2. to; extremes
3. by; means; of
4. for; the; sake; of
5. stage; fright

# Round 26

## I. Multiple Choice

| | | | | |
|---|---|---|---|---|
| 1. D | 2. A | 3. B | 4. C | 5. C |
| 6. A | 7. A | 8. D | 9. B | 10. C |
| 11. D | 12. B | 13. A | 14. D | 15. C |
| 16. A | 17. C | 18. D | 19. B | 20. B |

1. 要想健康長壽，你必須避免油膩食物。
   (A) 落後；(B) 強制實行；(C) 鉤住；**(D) 避免**

2. 該廣告誤導消費者，聲稱草本茶可使他們在一週內減掉十磅。
   **(A) 草本的**；(B) 絕對的；(C) 激烈的；(D) 種族的

3. 絕大多數人贊成近期的教育制度改革。
   (A) 不同種類；**(B) 大多數**；(C) 一堆；(D) 金額

4. 星期天晚起的想法對這名忙碌的職業女性很有吸引力。
   (A) 接著的；(B) 准許的；**(C) 有吸引力的**；(D) 欣賞的

5. 雖然這間餐廳的食物價格不菲，但因為服務好，我經常在那裡吃晚餐。
   (A) 干涉；(B) 觀察；**(C) 服務**；(D) 限制

6. 許多學者和知識分子聚集在會議室，談論一些教育問題。
   **(A) 知識分子**；(B) 行人；(C) 僕人；(D) 監護人

7. 學生們正在互相練習口說技巧，而老師則正在密切注視他們的進展。
   **(A) 密切注視**；(B) 暫停；(C) 撥號；(D) 批評

8. 如果 Chloe 答應在公共場合守規矩，她父親這週六就帶她去科學博物館。
   (A) 創造；(B) 使著迷；(C) 裝飾；**(D) 舉止端正**

9. 由於缺乏方向感，Nancy 經常在去一個新地方時迷路。
   (A) 榮耀；**(B) 感覺**；(C) 監督；(D) 一瞥

10. 當你說要辭職時，你是認真至極的嗎？
    (A) 心臟；(B) 意圖；**(C) 認真**；(D) 傾向

11. 男孩拉著他母親的襯衫袖子，說他想上廁所。
    (A) 圍巾；(B) (有帽舌的) 帽子；(C) 胸腔；**(D) 袖子**

12. 請倒多一點醬汁在義大利麵上。這樣會更好吃。
    (A) 劍；**(B) 醬汁**；(C) 皮革；(D) 優雅

13. 疾病是人類的敵人。
    **(A) 敵人**；(B) 出版社；(C) 設計師；(D) 傢伙

14. 這名老師有足夠的耐心，一遍又一遍地解釋這句話，直到每個學生都理解為止。
    (A) 糟糕的；(B) 遙遠的；(C) 凶猛的；**(D) 有耐心的**

15. Frank 在日曆上標記了他女朋友的生日，以防他忘記。
    (A) 習俗；(B) 歌劇；**(C) 日曆**；(D) 歷史

16. 起初，手機攜帶起來很笨拙，但它們現在卻輕巧多了。
    **(A) 笨拙的**；(B) 真誠的；(C) 合適的；(D) 高尚的

17. 申請人必須遵循申請簽證的正確程序。
    (A) 促銷；(B) 進步；(C) **程序**；(D) 準備

18. 這位學者對新的住房政策持批評態度。他認為這將導致房地產市場過熱。
    (A) 驕傲的；(B) 殘忍的；(C) 有抱負的；(D) **批評的**

19. 舊報紙的剪報使我想起我年輕時發生的那場可怕事故。
    (A) 想起；(B) **使想起**；(C) 記得；(D) 反映

20. 那名譯者做得很出色，她賺的每一分錢都是她應得的。
    (A) 要求；(B) **應得**；(C) 希望；(D) 加深

## II. Fill in the Blank

| 1. season | 2. memory | 3. blocked |
|-----------|-----------|------------|
| 4. Pluck  | 5. schedule | |

1. 這些桃子一定非常貴，因為它們不是當季了。
   ★ in/out of season (蔬果) 當季的 / 非當季的

2. 志工組織設立紀念碑以紀念強震中遇難的罹難者。★ in memory of sb 以紀念某人

3. 所有出村的道路都被敵人封鎖了。因此，村民無法拿到任何物資。★ block sth off 封閉…

4. 不要害怕。鼓起勇氣與對手戰鬥。
   ★ pluck up your courage 鼓起勇氣

5. 企劃案花了太多時間，以至於比計畫晚了幾週才完成。★ behind schedule 比預定時間晚

## III. Guided Translation

1. keep; an; eye; on
2. in; case
3. on; purpose
4. cover; up
5. fell; apart

# Round 27

## I. Multiple Choice

| 1. C | 2. C | 3. B | 4. D | 5. A |
|------|------|------|------|------|
| 6. A | 7. A | 8. B | 9. B | 10. D |
| 11. B | 12. D | 13. C | 14. A | 15. C |
| 16. C | 17. A | 18. D | 19. D | 20. B |

1. 電腦是一項革命性的發明。它改變了人們的生活方式。
   (A) 保守的；(B) 功能性的；(C) **革命性的**；(D) 流利的

2. 我沒有告訴 Fiona 那則壞消息，因為怕她會為此感到心煩。
   (A) 新鮮的；(B) 有機的；(C) **心煩的**；(D) 便利的

3. 對於工作進度緊迫的人來說，良好的時間管理是非常重要的。
   (A) 判斷；(B) **管理**；(C) 廣告；(D) 成就

4. 我想和 Miller 醫生預約今晚的門診，麻煩你。
   (A) 捐贈者；(B) 影響；(C) 解釋；(D) **預約**

5. 談話節目主持人的笑話令觀眾放聲大笑。
   (A) **大聲地說**；(B) 低語；(C) 恐慌；(D) 適應

6. 被控犯下強盜罪的男孩年僅 16 歲，應由少年法庭處置。
   (A) **搶劫**；(B) 創新；(C) 溪流；(D) 鞭韃

7. 有了適當的誘因，好奇心可以轉變為強大的學習動機。
   (A) **動機**；(B) 引文；(C) 懷疑；(D) 邀請

8. 那名球員隸屬於一個非常難加入的網球俱樂部。
   (A) 侷限；(B) **屬於**；(C) 借出；(D) 有關

9. Doris 打破平日的生活慣例。她沒去工作，反而去看了場戲。
   (A) 重力；(B) **慣例**；(C) 沉默；(D) 音調

10. 這個藥在五分鐘內就減輕了我的疼痛。我現在覺得好多了。
    (A) 忍受；(B) 經歷；(C) 改變；(D) **減輕**

11. 你遇到困難時不應該逃避，反而應該要面對並設法克服它們。
    (A) 收穫；(B) **困難**；(C) 商品；(D) 原料

12. 一些環保人士將會在這個週日發起反對使用塑膠吸管的活動。

(A) 觀念；(B) 投資；(C) 協商；(D) **活動**

13. 一架直升機被派去救援兩名山區的傷患。
    (A) 暖氣設備；(B) 約會；**(C) 直升機**；(D) 產業

14. 這位多產的作者過去五年來出版了十本以上的犯罪小說。
    **(A) 多產的**；(B) 僵硬的；(C) 醒目的；(D) 多愁善感的

15. 騎機車時記得戴上安全帽，以保護頭部。
    (A) 把手；(B) 小屋；**(C) 安全帽**；(D) 遺產

16. 該區種植的主要出口作物為咖啡和棉花。
    (A) 肌肉；(B) 微粒；**(C) 農作物**；(D) 車輛

17. Susan 不想結婚。她想要一輩子保持單身。
    **(A) 單身的**；(B) 匿名的；(C) 未受損的；(D) 孤立的

18. 村民們拼命嘗試阻止水壩的興建。
    (A) 基礎的；(B) 普遍的；(C) 民族的；**(D) 拼命的**

19. 天文學家的主要職責是觀察太空中的星體。
    (A) 危害；(B) 讓步；(C) 跟隨；**(D) 觀察**

20. Ray 是一個隨時準備好保衛國家的愛國公民。
    (A) 電影院；**(B) 公民**；(C) 黏土；(D) 常數

## II. Fill in the Blank

| 1. poured | 2. scenes | 3. fell |
|---|---|---|
| 4. presence | 5. booked | |

1. 哥哥潑了我的想法一頭冷水，說它完全行不通。★ pour cold water on sth 對…潑冷水

2. 兩位執行長擬定雙方企業的合併計畫，是以私下進行而非公開的方式。
   ★ behind the scenes 不公開地，幕後地

3. Marian 覺得很尷尬，因為她的笑話失敗了，完全沒有人笑。
   ★ fall flat (笑話、想法或建議) 未達到預期效果

4. 進行抽籤時，所有想讓孩子註冊該校的家長也都在場。★ in the presence of 在…面前

5. 令我們失望的是，這間旅館的房間在連假時段完全被預訂一空。★ book up 把…預訂一空

## III. Guided Translation

1. in; particular
2. blown; away
3. made; fun; of
4. as; soon; as
5. go; crazy

# Round 28

## I. Multiple Choice

| 1. A | 2. C | 3. A | 4. B | 5. D |
|---|---|---|---|---|
| 6. C | 7. D | 8. D | 9. B | 10. B |
| 11. B | 12. C | 13. B | 14. A | 15. D |
| 16. A | 17. D | 18. C | 19. C | 20. A |

1. 那隻蝴蝶迅速地和環境融為一體，以免遭到掠食者捕食。
   **(A) 迅速地**；(B) 有生產力地；(C) 明顯地；(D) 敏感地

2. 這些礦工使用的工具還很原始，所以很難提升他們的產量。
   (A) 進階的；(B) 壯麗的；**(C) 原始的**；(D) 科技的

3. 用餐禮儀會因文化而有所差異，所以建議照著當地人的方式做。
   **(A) 禮儀**；(B) 菜單；(C) 方法；(D) 措施

4. 午餐時間快到了，我們去找點東西吃吧。
   (A) 制訂；**(B) 接近**；(C) 相似；(D) 消耗

5. 殘忍的是，很多嬰兒和孩童在戰爭期間和父母失散。
   (A) 使氣餒；(B) 計算；(C) 宣布；**(D) 分開**

6. 每架班機起飛前，都要接受仔細的安全檢查。
   (A) 感染；(B) 注射；**(C) 檢查**；(D) 機構

7. 女王陛下有為數可觀被代代相傳的古董珠寶收藏。
   (A) 部分的；(B) 複合的；(C) 進步的；**(D) 古董的**

8. 我認為我從你寶貴的建議中獲益良多。
   (A) 損害；(B) 教育；(C) 強調；**(D) 獲益**

9. Black 先生從自己計畫的成功中得到滿足感。
   (A) 交易；**(B) 滿意**；(C) 遷徙；(D) 選舉

10. 地震災民看到他們倒塌房屋的殘骸，忍不住哭了出來。

(A) 體育運動；(B) **殘骸**；(C) 遵守；(D) 公民身分

11. 一般而言，移民必需通過考試才能取得美國公民身分。
(A) 保留；(B) **取得**；(C) 維持；(D) 給予

12. 校方在不讓任何一個孩子學習落後的前提下，展開了新的教學方案。
(A) 處方箋；(B) 妥協；(C) **前提**；(D) 消耗

13. 該名外交官保證會解決問題。他有信心能做出令人滿意的安排。
(A) 貢獻；(B) **解決**；(C) 誇大；(D) 進口

14. 瑪麗雪萊著的《科學怪人》被認為是科幻小說的首部作品。
(A) **小說**；(B) 論文；(C) 羅曼史；(D) 專輯

15. 如果我可以自己獨享一個寧靜的午後，我要看看小說，還要聽點輕音樂。
(A) 令人震驚的；(B) 嚇人的；(C) 寒冷的；(D) **寧靜的**

16. 如果你不知道該部門的分機號碼，可以打給接線生請他幫你轉過去。
(A) **分機**；(B) 說服；(C) 保護；(D) 解決辦法

17. Anita 對乳製品過敏，飲食中必須排除它們。
(A) 目的；(B) 猜謎；(C) 承諾；(D) **產品**

18. Jerry 的父母為了給他更好的教育，做了極大的犧牲。他們努力工作，好支付他的學費。
(A) 能量；(B) 誘惑；(C) **犧牲**；(D) 挫折

19. 雖然找到生還者的希望微乎其微，搜救行動仍在進行。
(A) 除非；(B) 以免；(C) **雖然**；(D) 關於

20. 該項調查揭露了 1970 年代亞洲的性別薪資差距。男性和女性在職場上的待遇並不平等。
(A) **職場**；(B) 大廳；(C) 後院；(D) 走廊

## II. Fill in the Blank

| | | |
|---|---|---|
| 1. possession | 2. credit | 3. notice |
| 4. bottom | 5. failed | |

1. 那名男子過海關時，被發現持有毒品並當場遭到逮捕。★ in possession of 擁有

2. 由於這對夫妻手頭上的錢不夠，他們決定貸款買車。★ on credit 信用貸款

3. 我們不可能在短時間內安排這麼盛大的晚宴。

★ on short notice 在短時間內

4. 關於這款智慧型手機的額外資訊，可以在網頁底部找到。★ bottom 底部

5. 結果證明，缺乏團隊合作對該計畫有致命影響。最後是以失敗收場。★ fail 失敗

## III. Guided Translation

1. To; my; surprise
2. over; and; over
3. used; to; be
4. far; from
5. goes; without; saying

# Round 29

## I. Multiple Choice

| | | | | |
|---|---|---|---|---|
| 1. B | 2. A | 3. C | 4. C | 5. D |
| 6. A | 7. B | 8. B | 9. D | 10. D |
| 11. D | 12. B | 13. C | 14. B | 15. C |
| 16. A | 17. C | 18. D | 19. A | 20. A |

1. James 夫婦看到兒子在畢業典禮上領到學位證書，感動到哭了出來。
(A) 梯子；(B) **學位證書**；(C) 監視；(D) 櫃檯

2. 我們詢問王教授當前的經濟局勢時，他有所保留且不願做任何評論。
(A) **評論**；(B) 職業；(C) 鏟子；(D) 陸龜

3. 這兩支隊伍明天會在體育館進行一場排球賽。
(A) 沉船；(B) 畫廊；(C) **體育館**；(D) 法庭

4. 大多數人認為這名建築師應為大樓的坍塌負責。
(A) 冒險；(B) 廣告；(C) **建築師**；(D) 螺絲

5. 救生員冒著自己的生命危險去救那個溺水的男孩。
(A) 防禦；(B) 位置；(C) 暴露；(D) **風險**

6. 別太在意 Michael 說的話。他說話經常都沒在考慮別人的。
(A) **認真地**；(B) 最近；(C) 輕輕地；(D) 合法地

7. 表演者設法掩飾他的緊張，但反而弄得更明顯。
(A) 原本的；(B) **明顯的**；(C) 細緻的；(D) 個別的

8. 明天的橄欖球賽因為颱風的關係取消了。門票將會退費。
(A) 執行；(**B**) **取消**；(C) 消失；(D) 通過

9. Phoebe 在我背後突然尖叫嚇了我一跳。
(A) 繞行；(B) 修理；(C) 禁止；(**D**) **驚嚇**

10. 因為太暗了， 我認不出那個黑暗中高高的人影。
(A) 田地；(B) 打架；(C) 柵欄；(**D**) **人影**

11. 屋裡有一股奇特的味道。它讓我感到不舒服。
(A) 充足的；(B) 親切的；(C) 神聖的；(**D**) **奇特的**

12. 人們可以在夜市嚐到各種異國口味的食物，像是泰式、義式還有日式。
(A) 臨床的；(**B**) **異國的**；(C) 嚴厲的；(D) 圖像的

13. 謠傳戰爭即將爆發，所以許多人正逃往其他國家。
(A) 趨勢；(B) 傳統；(**C**) **謠言**；(D) 機會

14. 既然你是初學者，我就給你一點如何投資股票的指導吧。
(A) 出價；(**B**) **投資**；(C) 彈跳；(D) 給予

15. 現今有許多年輕人想要投身法律界。他們相信當律師是個好賺的工作。
(A) 版本；(B) 傳播；(**C**) **職業**；(D) 保存

16. 東方和西方之間的文化有極大的差異例如信仰和習俗。
(**A**) **文化**；(B) 提示；(C) 捲髮；(D) 坐墊

17. Mina 將和前夫見面， 討論他們女兒的健康問題。
(A) 應付；(B) 保持；(**C**) **討論**；(D) 反轉

18. 我們鎮上的警長追查到那名謀殺超過 20 人的殺手的下落，終於解決了這起案件。
(A) 創辦人；(B) 牧羊人；(C) 祖先；(**D**) **警長**

19. 當 Eva 拒絕 Tommy 共享浪漫晚餐的邀約時，他感到很失望。
(**A**) **拒絕**；(B) 反抗；(C) 不同意；(D) 不贊同

20. 不用說我一定會比你早到那裡。我們來打個賭吧。
(**A**) **打賭**；(B) 依賴；(C) 聚焦；(D) 計算

## II. Fill in the Blank

| | | |
|---|---|---|
| 1. cheat | 2. cured | 3. deal |
| 4. lead | 5. consequences | |

1. 別聽那個男人的話。他像狐狸一樣狡猾，非常可能會欺騙你。★ cheat 欺騙

2. 病患經過適當治療， 終於在一年後治好了肺癌。★ cure sb of sth 治好

3. 那位導演的下部片將探討一名婦女和她不忠丈夫之間的關係。★ deal with sth 論述某事

4. 整場比賽 Steve 都保持領先， 沒有人有辦法追上他。★ take the lead 領先

5. Samuel 必須為他的行為承擔後果。
★ take the consequences 承擔後果

## III. Guided Translation

1. next; to; impossible
2. takes; for; granted
3. broke; down
4. out; of; place
5. brought; about

# Round 30

## I. Multiple Choice

| | | | | |
|---|---|---|---|---|
| 1. D | 2. A | 3. D | 4. C | 5. B |
| 6. A | 7. A | 8. A | 9. C | 10. C |
| 11. B | 12. C | 13. B | 14. D | 15. B |
| 16. A | 17. D | 18. D | 19. B | 20. C |

1. Ed 和 Mia 往往對持不同意見的人很不客氣 。因此，他們經常會吵起來。
(A) 幻想；(B) 關聯；(C) 組合；(**D**) **意見**

2. 到了晚上 11 點，那個男孩在母親的要求下不情願地回到他的臥室。
(**A**) **不情願的**；(B) 幸運的；(C) 有吸引力的；(D) 慷慨的

3. 這家連鎖咖啡廳的總公司位在臺北，分店則是遍布全臺。
(A) 外表；(B) 小喇叭；(C) 避難所；(**D**) **總部**

4. 這作者的新書至今幾乎沒引起社會大眾多少興趣。

(A) 產生；(B) 上升；(C) **引起**；(D) 飼養

5. 幸運地，在修車師傅的協助下，Isaac 的迷你廂型車終於又能動了，於是他得以繼續他的旅程。
   (A) 欺負；(B) **繼續**；(C) 使震驚；(D) 顯示

6. 隨著汽車的數量快速增長，近年來的道路交通量也大為增加。
   (A) **快速增長**；(B) 下降；(C) 清楚表達；(D) 分開

7. 除了我已經說過的這些，我沒有什麼要告訴你的了。
   (A) **在…之外**；(B) 在…下面；(C) 在…下方；(D) 在…後面

8. 阿里山以其美景聞名，尤其是壯麗的日出。難怪它會吸引那麼多遊客。
   (A) **景色**；(B) 宣傳；(C) 音量；(D) 定義

9. 圖書館非常安靜，只會偶爾聽到裡面學生的咳嗽聲。
   (A) (疾病) 末期的；(B) 真實的；(C) **偶爾的**；(D) 必要的

10. 為了降低全球的二氧化碳排放量，我們必須聚焦兩個基本領域：能源和農業。
    (A) 峽谷；(B) 獨木舟；(C) **碳**；(D) 帆布

11. 我需要一把剪刀來剪這條線。你可以幫我拿嗎？
    (A) 長筒襪；(B) **剪刀**；(C) 短襪；(D) 長褲

12. Nick 已從這起不幸的事件學到一課，即患難見真情。
    (A) 無疑地；(B) 幾乎不；(C) **意即**；(D) 可能

13. Jessica 在花園裡工作時，注意到有個奇怪的男子往她鄰居家偷窺。
    (A) 代替；(B) **窺視**；(C) 暈倒；(D) 猶豫

14. 我好奇得不得了。拜託告訴我比賽最後是誰贏了。
    (A) 敏感度；(B) 柔軟度；(C) 可信度；(D) **好奇心**

15. 我們的餐廳才剛設法撐了下來；還不確定什麼時候會開始賺錢。
    (A) 不可或缺的；(B) **賺錢的**；(C) 有益的；(D) 財務的

16. Grace 抱持決心追求她的人生目標。因此，我們都相信她有朝一日會成功。
    (A) **決心**；(B) 整合；(C) 總統職位；(D) 代理機構

17. 馬拉拉致力為女孩和年輕婦女爭取接受免費、完整教育的權利。
    (A) 捐贈；(B) 選擇；(C) 離開；(D) **專心致力**

18. 遇到緊急狀況時，我們應該保持頭腦冷靜。
    (A) 吊掛；(B) 失去；(C) 打擊；(D) **保持**

19. 在中國的帝制時期，龍通常會和強大的權力被聯想在一起。
    (A) 陪伴；(B) **聯想**；(C) 符合；(D) 押韻

20. 強烈颱風引起的土石流造成數十人死亡，以及更多人無家可歸。
    (A) 急迫的；(B) 需要照顧的；(C) **猛烈的**；(D) 聰明的

## II. Fill in the Blank

| | | |
|---|---|---|
| 1. solve | 2. brush | 3. searched |
| 4. degrees | 5. injured | |

1. Alfred 花盡心思去解數學題，希望得到好成績。
   ★ solve 解答

2. 在你去德國之前，我建議你重新複習一下你的德語。這樣你和當地人溝通會比較輕鬆。
   ★ brush up (on) sth 複習某事物

3. 警方搜索整個區域尋找失蹤的女子，但還是沒有找到任何線索。★ search 搜索

4. 努力工作讓那名工人的財務狀況漸漸好轉。
   ★ by degrees 逐漸

5. 那名警察穿了一件能夠防禦子彈的背心，這樣她在槍戰中就不會受傷。★ injure 受傷

## III. Guided Translation

1. dying; for
2. stands; to; reason
3. built; in/into
4. dines; out
5. took; refuge

三民網路書店
www.sanmin.com.tw

題本與解析本不分售
26-87239G